The
Lifeboat
at the
End
of the
Universe

Simon Brading

1

In the softly lit room an orgy was taking place. A dozen naked, impossibly beautiful young men and women were clustered in three close groups around two men and a woman in their mid-thirties. Equally naked, they weren't quite as good-looking as the others, but they were certainly not ugly. Those three, the crew members, were the centre of attention of their respective groups and were having every whim taken care of as they reclined on the profusion of throw cushions strewn on the thick carpet. There was no need for any words to be exchanged, though; the young men and women, Artificial Humans, or AHs, knew exactly what was wanted of them and had provided these services many times before - it was a part of their reason for existing. Consequently, the only sounds in the room were the soft music and the occasional groan or grunt of exertion or pleasure from the three crew members.

The dim lighting and the heavy velvet curtains hanging around the room created an intimate atmosphere perfectly suited to the carnal activities taking place and the aromas being gently wafted around the room along with a light cooling breeze only heightened the sensations of the participants. A few low tables covered with finger food, various liquids like chocolate and cream, and a variety of beverages, alcoholic as well as more refreshing, nourishing or invigorating ones, were set out around the room, safely out of the reach of the carelessly flailing limbs of the people engaged in the physical exertions.

Adam stood with his back to the wall a few metres away, decidedly over-dressed for the activities going on in the room, wearing a rather classically-cut black dinner jacket with trousers to match, a brilliant white dress shirt and a bow tie that matched the brilliant blue of his eyes. He was watching his charges with a smile on his face that was not in any way sexual, but was more one of avuncular indulgence.

It was impossible to tell his exact age; he had a timeless look to him that was quite unusual, but at the same time rather attractive and he

3

would have been more than welcome amongst the group. However, his task in these last hours was to make sure that the crew was getting exactly what they had wanted and he didn't have time to spend on his own enjoyment, although he could certainly afford to pause and savour a few brief moments of voyeuristic pleasure while he carried out his duties.

Satisfied that the three crew members were being entertained in the manner they had requested, he strode across the room, stepping carefully over entwined limbs and dodging the hands that reached for him.

He smiled gently and shook his head at the invitation in the crewwoman's eyes as he passed. The woman and he certainly weren't strangers, but this wasn't the time; he had a job to do. Her slight look of disappointment almost instantly disappeared as her eyes rolled up into her head and he paused to watch as she shuddered, moaning in delight as intense sensations of pleasure washed through her, stealing away all thoughts of him or of anything else for that matter.

He reached the far side of the room and pulled aside a curtain, revealing a blank white wall.

He took one final look back before passing through the door that slid out of his way, then letting the curtain fall back into place behind him to hide the writhing bodies.

He halted just inside the next room and took in the spectacle laid out before him, vastly different to the one that he had just witnessed.

This room was much larger than the previous one. It was a ballroom fit for a palace, and the setting was like something out of an old period drama. Handsome men and women in 19th century evening dress danced circuits around the floor as others looked on from the sides of the room, talking and laughing in loose groups while sipping champagne. Two large chandeliers hung overhead, shedding gentle light on the scene, while French windows opened out onto a patio where more couples were taking the night air. Music was provided by twelve musicians who sat at one end of the room on a raised platform.

While Adam watched, his jacket grew tails and his blue bow tie became a silk cravat of the same colour. His posture subtly changed as well as he straightened and lifted his chin to match the attitude of the other men. He judged his moment, making the necessary calculations, then stepped forward, switching places with a young man, an AH in a fanciful army uniform, who had been waltzing with a woman, doing it so expertly that she didn't even miss a step.

The woman was tall, in her late sixties, and handsome and the only real human in the room. Her dark hair was streaked with silver and she was wearing a white silk evening gown and pearls. Diamonds adorned her earrings and were scattered throughout her hair, sparkling in the candlelight, and the hair itself was done up in something that Marie Antoinette herself would not have been ashamed of.

They danced together, the smile never leaving Adam's face, nor his eyes from hers, and the woman laughed in delight as he spun her expertly around the floor.

'Oh, Adam, I'm going to miss this.'

Adam smiled even wider as he replied. 'No you won't, you'll be back before you know it.'

They had now completed half a circuit of the ballroom and were on the other side of the room from where he had entered. He gave her one last twirl before another AH, dressed as a prince of the Austro-Hungarian Empire, stepped in and took over just as smoothly as he had.

He walked to a nearby mirror on the wall and it swung aside silently for him, revealing another doorway with bright sunlight streaming through from the other side.

Adam stepped through the door, coming out of a tree and walked up a small hill to survey the situation.

Once again almost everybody on board had chosen something from the short "Romantic" period of human history back on Old Earth shortly before the expansion as their final entertainment and this scenario was no exception, albeit not a very common choice - a battle was taking place all around him and the noise was incredible as hundreds of men and machines fired a variety of weapons simultaneously.

A Mark IID Hurricane swooped directly overhead, its heavy cannon blazing, strafing a Panzer tank a hundred yards away. The tank exploded, spraying metal fragments in every direction and sending grey-clad men flying screaming through the air even as the Hurricane was pounced upon by a Messerschmitt, which sent it spinning into the ground. Men moved into the gap torn in their lines but were mowed down in turn by the fire coming from the machine gun emplacements they were attempting assault.

As Adam impassively watched the bloody fighting, a fictional representation of a battle that had never taken place, but which was replayed once every hundred thousand years to varying results, his coattails receded and his clothes changed shape and colour until in short order he was dressed in brown fatigues that were just a bit more stylish and well-fitted than was actually appropriate for the era. As a finishing touch, his cravat became a clerical collar, a religious symbol that would reportedly have provided a person with some safety in his passage across the battlefield. He didn't need it in the slightest, but he hadn't been able to resist injecting a little of his own sense of humour into so grim a setting (along with a dash of colour; he had left the collar a decidedly unauthentic blue).

He waited where he was, knowing that one of the two men he had come to see was fast approaching and didn't flinch when a Tiger tank squealed to a halt beside him, its treads missing him by inches. He turned to smile up at the commander in the turret, who took off his ear protectors and gave him a wide grin in return. The man was in his eighties, far too old to have actually commanded a tank in World War Two even if he hadn't been born many millions of years too late.

'How goes the battle, Generalfeldmarschall?' Adam spoke loudly, shouting over the noise of the fighting.

The man winked at him before he replied. 'I think, sorry, I *sink* zat I'fe got heem thees time!' His eyes widened and he ducked back into his tank as a near miss from a bazooka sprayed earth and stones up into the air to patter against the side of the tank. His head popped back out after the dirt had settled and he looked back down at Adam, who hadn't moved a muscle. 'Himmel! Zat vas a close vun! No more distractions, back to zee fun!'

'Have a good time, and keep working on the accent! It's still terrible!'

'Don't vorry, I vill! Forwards!!!'

The man gave the signal to go and the tank sprang forwards, down the hill towards the smoke obstructed ruins of a church sitting on the outskirts of a small French town. German tanks and soldiers were advancing slowly towards the building across the open ground all around Adam and the Tiger joined them in the fierce assault.

The church itself was occupied by a force of Allied soldiers who had taken up positions in the graveyard, facing the enemy. They had dug in as well as they could, creating machine gun emplacements surrounded by sandbags, earth ramparts and various freshly dug, but far too shallow, trenches. A row of coffins, which had been displaced by the earthworks, were respectfully placed against the church wall out of harm's way.

A constant stream of bullets created an almost physical link between the opposing forces, punctuated by bazooka fire that flared out from the defenders, occasionally destroying tanks, but more often giving the attackers a new hole in which to take cover. Overhead, Spitfires and Hurricanes were now dogfighting with ME109s and FW190s. One of the planes was burning, tumbling from the sky and it exploded on the ground amongst the attacking forces, the stink of burning aviation fuel joining the almost pleasant odour of fresh earth and the not so pleasant ones of charred flesh and spilt blood.

Adam strolled down the hill past the attacking forces and crossed their lines, once more stepping carefully over limbs, although the task was easier this time because most of them weren't moving nearly as much. He picked his way across the broken ground between the two forces, heedless of the death-dealing ammunition flying around him. An FW190 strafed the graveyard in front of the church, tearing British and American soldiers apart, and more earth was thrown up into the air, but Adam just walked through the chaos, completely unconcerned. He arrived at the Allied defences, went through a gap in the low wall of the cemetery, then walked calmly up and over the earthworks, jumping down the other side and into a trench to stand beside a silver-haired man, also in his eighties, dressed as a British Field Marshall and wearing a black beret on which had been pinned two cap badges. The man was crouched over, out of the fire, and shouting into a field telephone.

'Where are those damn tanks!?! I have two Panzer divisions bearing down on me! How the hell am I supposed to fight them off with Bazookas and Brownings?' As he listened to the reply he covered the mouthpiece and smiled up at Adam. 'What oh! I'll be with you in a second, old chap!'

Adam smiled and nodded, waving his assent, 'of course, please take care of business.' He turned his attention back to the battlefield, quickly and expertly surveying the Allied emplacements and the forces spread in front of them. It was going to be a close run thing even if the tanks arrived in time. The telephone was slammed back down on its receiver and he turned back to the Field Marshall with a raised eyebrow and an amused smile.

The man was red faced and angry, but spoke calmly to Adam. 'Sorry about that.'

Adam echoed his clipped British accent as he replied; all part of the entertainment. 'Don't mention it, old bean, I can see you have your hands full. So, are the Shermans going to get here on time?'

'They'd better bloody get here or I'll have Monty's guts for garters! And when they do we'll show these blighters what for!'

'Good show, good show! Well, I'll leave you to it. Toodle pip!'

'Tatty bye!' The Field Marshall turned back to his telephone and Adam climbed out of the trench and casually strolled away across the graveyard through the flying shrapnel of more explosions.

The wooden door of the church slid aside in a way that it wasn't originally supposed to do and let him pass.

Adam's clothes changed again, becoming a plain black suit over a blue shirt, as the door closed behind him and the sounds of explosions, screaming and gunfire were cut off immediately, which was a relief, no matter how illusory it had all been.

The room he found himself in was small and plain, longer than it was wide, and silent and empty except for a simple white bench along one of the light grey walls with a single row of metal pegs above it, each holding a simple white t-shirt and white cotton trousers on a white hanger.

Adam glanced at the items as he walked past, making sure that everything was in place, then went through the white door at the end, opposite where he'd come in.

Adam always felt good in this room, its white glow and the soft hum of the stasis pods comforted him somehow, made him feel that everything was right with the universe, even though he knew that it wasn't.

Ten empty stasis pods, soft white beds inclined at 45° with closed glass lids, were set in a semicircle opposite the door. In the centre of that semicircle stood a small tablet computer terminal on a stand, which lit up as Adam approached.

A graphical display of the pods appeared with relevant technical information below each one. A quick glance showed Adam that the pods were functioning correctly and ready to receive their occupants. The rest of the information was standard.

Stasis Group 82,457.
All systems nominal.
Time to stasis: 30:15 minutes.
Occupants will be notified in 20:15 minutes.

The timers continued to count down as he left the stand to walk around the pods, visually inspecting them; he didn't fully trust the computers and preferred to double check everything himself - he refused to cut corners as far as the lives of his charges were concerned. His inspection was thorough and he finished it at the exact same time as a chime sounded. He smiled to himself and went back to his place at the computer to wait.

Before too long the door slid open and the first of the crew members entered.

The tank commander was accompanied by a young couple, who still bore the flush of their exertions at the martial arts tournament they had been fighting in for a million years and wouldn't reach the final of for perhaps another million more. All three were all dressed in the white clothing that had been set out for them and all of them were barefoot. They nodded at Adam as they passed, going directly to their assigned pods and placing their hands on palm readers set into the lids. The glass swung up and the pods started to glow softly. Blue and inviting.

The door slid open again. This time it was the Field Marshall who walked in with the woman from the ballroom on his arm. They also nodded to Adam as they passed and went to the two pods in the centre of the semicircle, activating them, then joining hands, gazing into each other's eyes as if they were saying goodbye before a long journey.

The next group that came in were the two men and the woman from the orgy and they laughed, sharing a three-way kiss in the doorway before separating. As the woman went past, Adam reached out to take a champagne flute from her. He turned to put the glass down on the stand next to the computer and she pinched his arse while his back was turned, then laughed and skipped away to her pod.

The last two crew members came in only moments later: a man who still had his nose in a book, which he handed to Adam before going to his pod, and a woman who was carrying a flower. She held it to her nose one last time before giving it to Adam with a smile. Both items joined the champagne glass next to the computer.

Adam watched as the ten people got into their pods and laid down, his hand hovering ready over the screen. Couples waved to each other one last time and the woman from the orgy blew Adam a last, cheeky kiss before she rested her head back on the thin pillow of the bed.

He pressed a flashing icon and the hatches of the pods slowly closed, sealing with a hissing noise. Seconds later a sharp flash of blood red light came from each pod, filling the room, before fading quickly to a faint red glow.

The screen now displayed new information.

Stasis Group 82,457.
All systems nominal.
10 Occupants in residence.
Time to awakening: 99,999 years 273 days 23 hours 58:34 minutes.

The countdown started.

Satisfied, Adam took one last look at his charges, picked up the book, glass and flower, then left the room, mentally ticking off another successful *Recovery* period for one of the ten-person groups into which the millions of guests were divided on his ship, *Lifeboat NCXII275A*, from New California XII, as it wended its way across the universe.

The door hissed closed softly behind him.

ARCHIVE A3

Humanity-wide Retinal Broadcast from the President's office, New Earth. Eighty years until launch.

'Are these things on?'

The man behind the antique aluminium desk with the embossed presidential seal looked up at the men in grey suits lurking behind the scanners, receiving their almost panicked nods and waves for him to continue. 'Oh, OK, right. Er, hi guys! Bert Resten here, that's President Bert, I suppose. Some of you probably didn't know, but I won the lottery and I'm your President this year. Anyway, there's some important stuff they want me to tell you and that's why we're doing this emergency retinal broadcast thingy. Sorry about that, I really hope you weren't doing anything important.'

The image of the President was being broadcast simultaneously across every world that humanity had infected, reaching all of the neighbouring galaxies to which they had spread over the last billion or so years (nobody was quite sure exactly how long it had been, they had given up counting) and every single member of the human race had his image projected directly onto their retina by the implants which had been given to newborn babies for the last few million years as standard.

Most people stopped what they were doing to give him their full attention, whether they were working, sleeping, playing, eating, it didn't matter; universal retinal broadcasts were highly unusual, a rare and special occurrence only used in an emergency. The last broadcast had been over four hundred years ago in fact, when there had been an alien-life sighting. It had quickly turned out to be hoax, just like all the rest had been, but not before it had embarrassed the hell out of the already-celebrating scientific community. Their enthusiasm to announce the discovery of alien life had been more than understandable though; in all the human race's years of exploration and expansion throughout the nearby galaxies, against all reasonable expectations, *not once* had life beyond the range of that available on Earth been found.

The President continued. 'Yeah, well, folks, it's like this. There are some really clever science guys here on New Earth who have been telling me some crazy stuff the last couple of days since I moved into the Grey Manse here. Basically, they've told me we're coming to the end of our stay in this universe. They say that it's collapsing at a quicker rate all the time and that's why we've been having all these quakes and freaky weather and stuff everywhere.'

He licked his lips and glanced at the men behind the scanners for reassurance. He didn't receive any, but continued anyway. 'Now, before you all go out and panic like I did, they say that it's OK for now and we've got a long time, like a few billion years or so before things really start to get hairy. But they also say that if we're going to try to do something about it then we have to do it now, like, right away. Anyway, just giving you all the heads up. If you want to know more about it then there's all sorts of stuff they've put together that you can tune your implants into and take a look at. Frankly, I don't understand the half of it, but maybe you will. Well, anyway, that's it for now, um, I suppose someone will get back to you when there's a plan or something; I know they're working on one, but they haven't told me about it yet. So, uh, just chill for now I suppose and watch this space! Bye!'

2

Adam stood in the changing room, just outside the door of the stasis room. The door turned red behind him and he waited while the ship ran through its processes, monitoring them in his mind while he watched men and women, AHs, come in and take away the clothes and other items the previous Stasis Group had left behind, leaving the room empty and once again spotless. When they were gone he took off his tie, folding it and putting it in his pocket as his jacket, shoes and trousers faded and turned white, the cut of them changing, becoming looser, less fashionable and more functional. In seconds the smart host was gone and in his place was a doctor, a familiar and comforting image - the first thing every Stasis Group saw when they woke.

Everything was ready. He nodded in satisfaction and turned in place just as the door pulsed green before fading back to its normal white, then slid open silently.

The white room containing the stasis pods looked exactly the same as it had before but was in fact an entirely different room, with ten different people waiting to be woken in ten different pods and a subtly different report on the tablet screen.

Stasis Group 82,458.
All systems nominal.
10 Occupants in residence.
Time to awakening: 0 years 0 days 0 hours 0:15 minutes.

As the timer counted down, the red lights of the pods slowly faded through pink to white and when it reached zero a soft chime sounded and the hatches smoothly swung up.

The group of ten people who would form the crew for the next three months woke up as if from a deep sleep.

This was something that always amused Adam; there was no perceivable gap between waking periods for stasis subjects and hibernation in this way appeared instantaneous for the person, but the human body still insisted on running through its little mechanisms and habits, tricking the occupants into thinking that they had been asleep instead of frozen. The people were scratching faces or running their hands through hair that hadn't moved a millimetre since they were last awake, feeling for changes that rationally they knew couldn't have taken place, but that they still, irrationally, felt the need to check for. They glanced from side to side, looking at adjacent pods and smiling at partners and friends, making sure they were there. Gestures that Adam reflected were totally unnecessary and very human.

Almost immediately they started to sit up and step out of the pods.

A middle-aged couple were first on their feet and they reached out to join hands, smiling and kissing as they passed Adam on the way out of the room. Two women paused next to their beds to embrace each other and kiss before they too left. The rest of the crew members followed in a loose group, eager to get back to their lives and not waste a single moment of the all too short time allotted to them, all except for one man, who came to a halt beside Adam. He was tall, in his mid-forties, dark haired and good-looking in a ruggedly-handsome kind of way, he wasn't smiling and didn't seem as happy to be awake as everyone else had been.

'Hi, Adam, long time no see.'

Adam smiled. 'Hi, Tom. Well, it has been a hundred thousand years, but it should only have been an instant for you. Has there been a malfunction in your pod? Let me check that out for you...'

The smile on Adam's face was gone for the first time and replaced by a serious expression as he started to tap on the screen, bringing up a diagnostic of Tom's pod. He started flicking rapidly through long lines of numbers and statistics before Tom stopped him with an exasperated sigh. 'It was just a figure of speech, Adam. Didn't your programmers teach you any of those?'

Adam stopped typing and looked up at him in surprise. 'Ah, of course. I'm sorry, Tom, I was thinking of my responsibilities; they take first priority over humour I'm afraid, and I didn't realise.'

'Yeah, of course not... Catch ya later.' There was a note of distrust in Tom's voice, but his expression was completely unreadable as he turned and walked out of the room.

Adam smiled at him, but Tom didn't see it when the door slid closed and hid him from sight.

Adam turned back to the computer and returned to the main information screen.

Stasis Group 82,458.
All systems nominal.
Time to stasis 0 years 90 days 23 hours 57:45 minutes.
Occupants will be notified in 0 years 89 days 23 hours 47:45 minutes.

He took one last look around the room, then left.

ARCHIVE A23

Humanity-wide Retinal Broadcast.
Sixty years until launch.

For the second time in recent history, humanity in its entirety was brought up short by a broadcast from New Earth. This time they had been given notice that it was coming, so it didn't come as so much of a shock and caused far less accidents.

A man with a mellow voice narrated the broadcast, which showed a fly-by of a computer-generated wire-frame model of a space ship being constructed in a space dock orbiting a blue and green planet.

'Hello, my name is Adam Goodwin and I am responsible for the design and concept of what we are coming to call the "Lifeboat" program.

'Here you can see the design of the ship that we've settled upon; a standard cone shape that has comfortable living quarters in the nose, leaving the vast majority of the rest of the ship to be almost entirely dedicated to storage for the passengers. Each Lifeboat will be capable of carrying up to four million people in stasis pods and will be equipped with a crew of two hundred Artificial Human servants to aid with servicing the ship and provide entertainment during scheduled Recovery periods. The ships will have the most advanced propulsion systems that we have constructed to date and will be able to indefinitely sustain a cruising speed approaching that of light.'

The transmission continued as the wire-frame was slowly built on until it was complete, revealing a pearlescent white conical spaceship, slick, sleek, with no windows and almost no protrusions.

'The design is similar to that of early colony ships, but on a much larger scale. As they will be travelling individually and not as part of a fleet, each ship needs to have the materials, both genetic and physical, necessary to establish an outpost.

'Time is of the essence, so effective immediately, every current human colony is under orders to construct as many Lifeboats as they can, as fast as they can, launching them as soon as they are ready, in order to maximise the possibility of survival.'

The completed ship left the space dock and its engines ignited. It quickly left the planet behind and disappeared into the darkness of space. It was replaced by a logo; the silhouette of the ship picked out in white on a royal blue background, surrounded by a ring of white stars. Underneath was written the single word "Hope".

'The Lifeboats will be sent out on varying trajectories into the universe in the hope that they can escape the coming Big Crunch and survive the ensuing Big Bang in order to spread a new wave of humanity across the new worlds that will form in time. It's a long shot, but it's the best chance humanity has. Thank you, and best of luck.'

3

Adam stood in the doorway and looked around the common room, making sure that everything was ready and in place for the welcome back dinner.

The common room was a moderately-sized cube, precisely twenty-three point five metres each side, decorated with soft soothing colours - the only room in the living quarters section of the ship that wasn't predominantly white or some shade of grey. In the middle of the room was a single oblong table, with eleven chairs but only ten place settings. A buffet was set up against the wall on one side next to the entrance and behind it stood five motionless men and women, AHs, dressed in white chef's uniforms. On the other side of the table, directly across from the door, were various comfortable sofas and armchairs set in a loose circle.

Satisfied that all was as it should be, Adam took off his jacket and deposited it in the repository that opened up for him in the wall next to the door, then moved across the room. His trousers had already gone back to their previous black and the shirt to its light blue, and as he walked he unbuttoned his sleeves and rolled them up; it was time to present a more informal aspect. He stood behind the chair at the head of the table, the one without a plate or cutlery, and rested his hands on its back, instantly freezing in place, suddenly as unnaturally motionless as the servers behind the buffet.

He became active again not long after when the door slid open and the crew members wandered in, but didn't move from his place or posture, instead just waited patiently for them to fill their plates and get drinks.

The men and women were all dressed in the simple jackets and trousers that served as the ship's unofficial uniform, but each wore different colours according to their own preferences.

Jacob, a white-haired man in his sixties with quite long hair and wearing an off-white jacket, led them in, rushing to the buffet. 'How is

it that every time I wake up I'm hungrier than the last? I'm starving!'
He grabbed a plate and started to fill it, putting as much food into his
mouth as he did on the plate.

A woman in her fifties, Barbara, followed him to the buffet,
although rather more sedately; she was heavily pregnant with a very
noticeable bulge under her pastel purple jacket. She answered him in a
southern drawl while she shadowed him, filling her plate in a more
dignified manner. 'Well, sugar, I'm sure it's all in your mind, but now
you come to mention it I'm feeling a mite peckish myself. I thought
that wasn't possible, but maybe it's because I'm eating for three!' She
motioned for one of the servers to fill a glass with juice for her, then
followed Jacob to the table.

Richard, a handsome but soft-looking man wearing brown, also in
his fifties, had overheard their conversation. 'I'm sure it's just in your
pretty head. I can examine it for you, if you'd like?' He sat down next
to Barbara and they leant together to kiss, chastely, then he pulled back
and rubbed his hand gently over her swollen belly with a smile.

'Hey! It's *my* job to assess our mental health and I think I might be
crazy… for you!' She answered him, putting her hand over his.

'Get a room!' A young man, Leo, barely out of his teens and wearing
a white jacket, screwed up his face in mock disgust and jokingly told
them off.

A girl, Rachel, about the same age as Leo and dressed in red, sat
down next to him and nudged him in the ribs. 'Oh, leave them be, one
day *we'll* probably be like that!'

'Or maybe it's *us* who will be like that!' Another young girl, Tammy,
dressed in a painfully bright, pink jacket, sat down on the other side of
Leo and pulled him towards her. The three of them shared smiles and
amorous looks.

'Oh, please, can't we just eat in peace for once?' Tom was dressed
in black and he stared across the table at them with an annoyed
expression. He had taken a place at the end of the table, as far away
from Adam as he could get.

The three youths exchanged playful glances, then simultaneously
stuck their tongues out at him.

The whole group laughed except for Tom, who did his best to
ignore them and continued eating.

Adam observed them all closely, noting the little changes in their
behaviour from what was normal for them. Stasis affected everyone
slightly differently; most people became euphoric, hungry, or horny,
like nine of the people sitting at the table in front of him, but Tom,

who was always rather annoyed with everyone and everything around him, had that trait exaggerated for the first hours after awakening. It was nothing that Adam felt that he had to worry about, though, and he smiled and took advantage of a momentary break in the conversation to get his necessary business out of the way. 'I take it that none of you are feeling any ill effects from the hibernation?'

Jacob answered around a mouthful of food. 'I'm *really* hungry!'

Tom gave Jacob an exasperated look, but Adam just smiled indulgently. 'Aside from feeling hungry, does anyone have any other complaint that *actually* warrants attention from Sarah or Elaine?' He indicated a couple of very good-looking women in their late twenties who acted as the group's doctor and nurse.

There were various negative sounds and motions from everyone around the table as they took full advantage of the interruption to continue to eat, shovelling food into their mouths as if they hadn't eaten for a long time, which, of course, they hadn't.

Adam smiled. 'Good! Then I'll give you a quick update on the current situation. First of all, let me wish all of you a happy birthday! Due to the effects of relativity you are now more than a billion years old!'

There were cheers and laughter from most of the group and the three youngest members whooped and high-fived.

Adam waited patiently for the group to settle down again, smiling all the while and when there was quiet he caused a holographic projection to spring into life over the middle of the table, simultaneously dimming the lights slightly.

The projection showed first the white conical form of the Lifeboat, parts of it alternately glowing green as it slowly rotated about its axes. 'As you can see all ship's systems are functioning nominally. Nothing has worn out or broken in the last hundred thousand years.'

The Lifeboat seemed to burst apart as an uncountable number of galaxies, novas, nebulae, interstellar dust and patches of darkness flew past the crew members to take up positions around the room, becoming a model of the known universe. A small golden triangle hovering high above the table showed the position of their Lifeboat relative to the various astronomical bodies and it was joined by a sea of millions of similar icons in green that showed the positions of the other Lifeboats in the fleet. It was an incredible complex and detailed model, far too much for anybody to properly take in. Anybody human anyway.

Superimposed on the table in front of them were two displays, one that was labelled "Ship Time" and the other that said "Relative Time". The display showing the ship's time was ticking up a second at a time but the other, the one that represented the time passing in the surrounding universe, was orders of magnitude higher, surpassing it by more than a billion years, and the seconds, minutes and hours were rolling around much faster, so fast that they were an unreadable blur.

Adam loved this part of his wake-up presentation; it always impressed the hell out of the people who saw it and he gave them a little time to take in the scale of what they were looking at before he continued. He waved a hand at the green dots in the middle of the hologram and a handful of them turned red. 'Unfortunately, we have lost contact with some of the other Lifeboats, but there is no need to worry; there are many possible causes for the loss of contact with a Lifeboat and it does not *necessarily* mean that it has been destroyed.'

There was a short silence as the group heaved a collective sigh; they knew that this venture was a risky one at best, but even so, the destruction, or possible destruction of a Lifeboat represented a huge loss of human life and a reduction in the hope for the continuation of the species. It was enough to give them a reason to mourn, if only for a moment.

A pulsing golden line began to stretch out in front of the icon representing their Lifeboat, bringing their attention back to the display. It slowly sketched a path through the tiny galaxies and other obstacles in their path and made its way over their heads towards the corner of the room and the blurry edge of the hologram.

'Our course remains clear and there appear to be no serious problems or obstacles ahead of us in the foreseeable future. The edge of the universe is not within scanner range yet and we still have no idea what will be waiting for us there. So, in summary, there has been no change while you were sleeping - we have a long way to travel, but everything is going well so far.'

Adam finished his presentation and the lights in the room came back up as the holographic projection evaporated. The group, which had been transfixed by the beauty of the model above them, now returned their attention to their food and only half-listened to the remainder of his speech; this wasn't their first briefing and their interest had all but disappeared along with the light show.

'Tom will be compiling a more detailed report over the next few weeks as part of his duties and, as the resident Astrophysicist on board, he will be able to answer any questions you might have much better than I can.'

He paused and looked around the room. Predictably the three youths were completely ignoring him, talking and giggling amongst themselves, and both couples, Richard and Barbara, and Elaine and Sarah, only had eyes for each other. John, an eighty-year-old silver-haired gentleman and the resident historian, already had his nose back in his book as he ate.

The only person who had paid absolute attention throughout his whole speech and who still had his gaze fixed firmly on him was Tom.

'Well, thank you all for your kind attention. Get a good night's rest and I will see you all on the beach tomorrow for the compulsory, but ever so delightful, R and R. Don't forget your swimwear!'

Adam gave the group a last big smile, seen only by Tom, then pulled his chair out and sat down.

Very soon, everybody had finished eating and began to stand and drift away, leaving the room in their couples and threesomes, or in the case of Jacob and John, on their own.

Tom was the only one who remained behind, sitting, thinking. Staring at Adam.

Adam met his eyes without blinking.

They stayed like that for several seconds, more than long enough to make any human uncomfortable.

Eventually, Tom pushed back his chair and left the room without saying a word or looking back.

Adam watched him go and as soon as the door closed behind him the smile vanished from his face to be replaced by a look that was as close to concern as Adam's face ever wore.

4

Adam liked to call this place his "Sanctum Sanctorum" and he was the only being on the ship, human, mechanical, or otherwise, who could access it, or even knew of its existence.

The room was totally blank, spherical and coloured a uniform light grey, the only feature was a white padded chair on a swivel. The arm of the chair had a computer screen on it which lit up as he entered the room and he was already typing on it as he sat down.

Dozens of images in ten separate groups sprang into being in the air around him, showing various views of bedrooms and bathrooms, each group of which was labelled with the name of one of the crew members.

Adam scanned them quickly, seeing that the rooms labelled "Leo" and "Tammy" were empty because both of their assigned occupants were in Rachel's room. Similarly Barbara was in Richard's room and Sarah was in Elaine's room.

He pressed a few icons on the screen and the views of the empty rooms disappeared. The remaining images rearranged themselves in the air in front of him and grew larger to fill the space that had been vacated.

Barbara and Richard were cuddled up together, already asleep and Adam smiled when he saw that Richard's arm was protectively cradled around Barbara's bulge.

He wasn't at all surprised to see that the three youths were having energetic sex.

Jacob was cross-legged on the floor, meditating, a large marijuana joint already waiting for him.

John was reading. No surprise there.

Sarah and Elaine were chatting, sharing a bottle of wine between them. They made a good couple, in and out of the sick bay.

The only person not resting was Tom and Adam brought the views of his room to the front and enlarged them.

The astrophysicist was pacing up and down in his room, thinking. He came to some conclusion and moved to pick up a tablet computer from his bedside table. A few taps and the projection of the universe that Adam had shown the crew members earlier filled his room.

He walked around and through it, studying it.

Adam sat in his chair and watched him, unsmiling.

ARCHIVE E2

Prime time talk-show Una's Universe.
Thirty-five years until launch.

Two people sat in armchairs on a small stage in front of an array of scanners. It was the typical talk-show set-up that hadn't changed since the beginning of the television era.

The host, Una Thorpe, a soberly dressed young woman with long, straight, dirty-blond hair, was interviewing Dr Adam Goodwin, who was now being called "the Father of the Lifeboat Project". Dr Goodwin had silver hair and looked to be in his seventies, but had a sharp focus and a youthful glint in his eyes as he spoke.

'For a comparatively short time, a few hundred years or so, the human race made huge leaps forward in technological advancement, taking to the stars and spreading across the galaxy in their search for anyone, anything, any *being* different to us. We sent colonising missions to all the nearby galaxies, and then to the ones that weren't so near, but time after time we came up empty-handed. We persisted for a while, but eventually it became all too clear that there was nothing to keep searching for, no life beyond what was on our own Earth. We have detected no signals, found no signs, had no surprise archaeological finds. Humanity has had to accept with a, let's say, ninety-eight percent probability, that we are utterly alone in the universe.

'Because of that there was no longer anything for us to strive towards, nothing to keep us moving forwards or motivate us. There is no external threat to us and with the abolishment of war among ourselves, nothing to stimulate or necessitate further growth, with the consequence that we have been living the same way for billions of years and have grown extremely comfortable - expansion has stopped, technology has stagnated, our population is controlled, there are no shortages of resources, our Artificial Humans do everything for us, we have power cells that last for all time... Even when our suns go nova we just pick up our planets and move to the next one!

'This endeavour is humanity's last great leap forward into the unknown, our last adventure. A return to the pioneering spirit of aeons past which has stimulated one last evolutionary step before we again succumb to ennui.'

As Dr Goodwin took a sip of water the hostess took advantage of the pause to ask a question. 'That doesn't explain why there is only now such a big panic to escape. Couldn't something have been done about this before? Prevented it maybe?'

Dr Goodwin nodded enthusiastically as he swallowed. 'Undoubtedly a more elegant solution could have been found in time, human ingenuity is such that I'm positive of it. The problem is that we all of us forgot that this was going to happen.'

Una blinked. 'I'm sorry?'

'It seems that, even in the days before we left our original solar system, scientists knew that one day this could happen, that the *Big Crunch* was a distinct possibility, if not a certainty. However, it always seemed so far away, in such a far distant future, that it was all but impossible to conceive of and pointless to plan for. So we stopped keeping an eye out and somebody, somewhere, forgot to press a button, or write a program, or set an alarm to remind us to do something about the situation. I'm sure you know how it is.'

'Actually, the studio always sends someone to wake me up.'

Dr Goodwin dutifully laughed at the hostess' joke.

'So why do we have to go right now? Surely the end of the world is still a very long way away? In his historical address to the human race, President Resten said, and I quote: "we've got a long time, like a few billion years or so before things really start to get hairy." Why is there such a hurry all of a sudden?'

'I won't bore you with the details, but it's all to do with the distances. Due to our quantum communications breakthroughs we take for granted that we have instant communication with anyone, no matter how far away they are, even in another galaxy. To all intents and purposes our words travel infinitely faster than the speed of light. But while our communications are instantaneous our methods of travel certainly are not; we ourselves are limited to speeds that approach, but don't quite reach the speed of light.

'To escape the Big Crunch we have to get far enough past the edge of the universe that we are unaffected by the gravitational effects, and currently the edge of the universe is calculated as being at about fifty billion light years from us, which means that light would have to travel fifty billion years to get to it.'

'Wow. That's quite a long time.'

'Indeed, so it would seem that we have plenty of time. However, it all becomes much more complicated when things like relativity and the rate of collapse are figured into the equation. The inescapable reality is that we have to leave *now* if we are to have *any* chance of surviving at all. In fact we might already be too late.'

The hostess had turned slightly white as the seriousness of the situation sank in finally. They sat in silence for a couple of seconds, before the woman turned to the camera. Her voice broke slightly as she spoke, forcing a smile. 'OK, we'll be back after a short break, please don't go anywhere!'

5

Adam stood on the white sand with his back to the ocean, waves of clear blue water lapping on the gently sloping beach behind him. He was absolutely still, a welcoming smile fixed on his face, as he waited for the crew members to arrive.

He was wearing an awful Hawaiian shirt - a clash of pink flamingos wading in pastel blue water and shaded by green palm fronds - which flapped slightly in the gentle breeze, open over a bright yellow tank top, with red and white Bermuda shorts and dark blue flip-flops. There was a line of pink zinc sunblock under each of his blue eyes and down the top of his pale nose.

To one side of him a volleyball court was set up in the sand, while on the other there was a wooden hut that served as a bar, inside which a gorgeous Hawaiian woman, an AH, with flowers in her hair and wearing only a grass skirt, stood equally motionless, ready to serve. Beach loungers were set out in front of the bar, facing the sea. Further down the beach was a line of small, but well-appointed, wooden bungalows sitting a little way back from the water in the shade of the line of palm trees marking the edge of the nearby jungle. The water itself was flat and calm in the protection of a bay which was almost, but not quite, enclosed by spits of sand and trees, and the ocean beyond stretched out to a horizon that seemed infinite.

The only sounds were those of the waves as they broke softly on the sand, the gentle hiss as they drew back and the occasional call of a bird of paradise gliding overhead.

The setting was idyllic in the extreme and it had been specifically designed to be most people's idea of paradise; the ideal place for the crew to relax and recover when first waking from hibernation.

Adam blinked and unfroze as a door appeared seemingly in thin air in front of him, sliding open to reveal Rachel and Tammy, dressed in bikinis and sarongs and carrying small bags, followed closely by Leo.

Adam nodded in greeting as Rachel and Tammy squealed and ran past him. They dropped their bags and sarongs on loungers, then charged straight down the beach and splashed into the water. Leo followed them, smiling, a little slower and more dignified, but no less enthusiastically.

The rest of the group were not far behind the trio and the door remained open as they entered. Richard helped Barbara straight to a lounger, her bulge covered demurely by a loose shirt. Sarah and Elaine also went straight to the loungers and Sarah immediately bent to examine Barbara, asking her how she had slept, while Elaine went to the bar for drinks, coming back shortly with fruit juice for the four of them.

Jacob was next to appear, wearing an extremely small set of swimming briefs and nothing else. He walked past Adam, dropped his bag on the sand and put his hands on his hips as he turned his face up to the sun. 'Far out, man.' He sat down near the water's edge and folded himself into the lotus position, took a spliff out of his bag and lit up.

Tom and John were the last people through the door. They were deep in conversation, but split up shortly after they stepped onto the beach. As the most conservative of the group they were wearing short-sleeve shirts and shorts.

John dropped his bag on a lounger and took his shirt off before going down to the water and diving straight in.

Tom, however, headed straight to the bar and hopped onto a stool. 'Whisky, rocks.' He pushed his hat, a brown Stetson that wasn't strictly beachwear, up his forehead a bit as he waited, picking at a bowl of nuts.

The AH smiled at him and handed him his drink. Tom immediately downed it. 'Another.' In short order he had another drink in his hand and he swivelled around on the stool and leant back against the bar, surveying the group critically. He grimaced at the trio who were now laughing and splashing each other, then at Jacob who was already surrounded by a cloud of aromatic smoke.

Adam wandered over to join Tom at the bar, sitting down next to him. 'Do you want a paper umbrella in that?'

'Huh. Funny.' Tom wasn't amused.

'You know that the whole point of this is for you to enjoy yourself for a few days and to shake off the effects of the stasis.'

'Of course I do.'

'Then I don't understand why you act like this every time. You know you're going to start enjoying yourself sooner or later, you always do. If you understand the need, the *necessity* of this, then why don't you just accept it and have fun right from the start?'

'Because I'd rather just be left alone for now, mental health be damned. Nobody will be able to tell the difference when I'm drunk anyway, except for me.' He saluted Adam with the glass and downed the remains before turning back to the bar and signalling for another. The barmaid handed it to him and he hunched over the bar, pointedly ignoring Adam.

Adam smiled indulgently, then got off the stool and went to the group that was gathered around the pregnant Barbara. If Tom wanted to be left alone with his irrationality then he would leave him alone, at least for the moment.

ARCHIVE E17

Talk-show Good Morning, Humanity! With Carl Craven. *Special edition, from construction yard gamma in geosynchronous orbit around New Earth. Twenty years until launch.*

Dr Adam Goodwin sat in front of a floor to ceiling glass window. There was a walking stick leaning against his chair, and he looked much older than he had done in his first public appearance fifteen years previously on the *Una's Universe* talk show. His silver hair was now white and his face was deeply lined, especially his forehead; the stress of running such a vast and important project was obviously taking its toll. Behind him, in the far distance but still filling most of the window, could be seen the huge conical shape of a Lifeboat. It was still in the early stages of construction, not much more than a metal framework and a few white panels surrounded by flimsy looking scaffolding. It was illuminated by powerful spotlights and was the only object that could be seen; the rest of the view was taken up by the absolute black of open space. The window served as the backdrop for the talk show and a holographic sign over the window proudly proclaimed *"Good Morning, Humanity!* Special edition, brought to you by *Universoda!"*

Dr Goodwin was with two other people. To his left sat Rita Lensworth, a middle aged woman in a very bright and shiny purple dress with a huge smile on her face who was the project-wide Entertainment Consultant. On the other side of her was the male host of the program, Carl Craven. He was young, dressed in a royal blue dinner jacket and bow tie over a black shirt and white trousers and had a permanent smile under his impressively coiffed blue-black hair. He was very obviously one of those talk show hosts who were popular more for their looks and entertainment value rather than their intelligent discourse.

The entire show had been dedicated to the Lifeboat project and Craven had just finished interviewing a few of the other people involved, including the Budget Supervisor for the New Earth construction effort, who had turned out to be a very boring, not at all photogenic little man, who hadn't provided anything in the way of entertainment. Not even the general enthusiasm for the project had been able to keep the ratings up and Craven was hoping to end on a much higher note with his final guests.

'Now, I understand from our sources that there will be extensive leisure facilities aboard the Lifeboats.' Craven smiled obsequiously. 'We've already heard that each ship will have a crew of Artificial Humans providing for their every, ahem, *need*, and that they will also be taking a database with the collected literary works of the entire human race. But I assume that the passengers aren't going to be limited to just having sex and reading books for billions of years! So, what else can they look forward to?'

Dr Goodwin opened his mouth to answer, but he was interrupted by Rita, who laughed in an annoyingly bubbly manner before speaking. 'Why, that's the best part of the whole deal! Each of the Lifeboats will be fitted with the very latest in *Holo Room* capabilities, and even though the use of them will be strictly rationed, they are capable of recreating any environment, with millions of scenarios preprogrammed before launch.'

'You say their use will be strictly rationed? Is that necessary?'

'Of course! They drain an awful lot of power, more than can be compensated for by the ship. So, to prevent any permanent power loss they will only be used for a few hours a month at the most.'

'Then why, may I ask, have them at all? Surely the power and space would be better used for something else, I don't know, like the engines, or the environmental systems?'

'Silly! Those things are more than taken care of! Dr Goodwin has seen to it that there are multiple redundancies in place and those systems have a *Forever Guarantee*! No, the Holo Rooms are one of the most important parts of the ship, essential for the well-being of the passengers, or should I say, the "Crew"; they will be used during the two hours immediately before entering stasis. It's very, very important to bring up endorphin levels before entering stasis.'

Craven blinked, puzzled. 'Endorphins? Are you taking endorphins with you? I thought animal species were only going as DNA samples…'

Dr Goodwin face-palmed and shook his head. '*Endorphins*, not *dolphins*, you…' He sighed and cut himself off with a supreme effort. He really didn't like doing these kinds of lowbrow talk shows, but he had let himself be convinced that they were an essential part of convincing the human race of the necessity of the Lifeboats, of reassuring them that they were going to be safe and well taken care of once they were on board.

Rita giggled and put her hand on Dr Goodwin's arm, stroking it gently in a familiar manner and he glanced down at it in something approaching horror as she answered Craven's question. 'Thank you, Adam. *Endorphins*, Carl. High levels of endorphins are essential because they help to protect the mind from damage during stasis, otherwise so-called "stasis psychosis" could occur.'

'That's very interesting, Rita and maybe we could come back to that later, but I wanted to talk about these reports we've been getting that there is a beach on board the ship. Surely that can't be true?'

'Of course it is! You see, when you come out of stasis, those levels of dolphins…'

'Oh, for pity's sake…' Dr Goodwin was slumped into his seat, desperately trying not to show the shame he was feeling at having to share the broadcast with his fellow "expert".

'Oh yes, endorphins! Sorry, Dr A!' Rita giggled and patted Dr Goodwin on the arm again, before he could snatch it away. 'Yes, so, these endorphins get really low again when people come out of stasis and while the Holo Rooms are a great way to give their levels a short boost, it's not sufficient for the long term. Which is where the beach comes in - each Lifeboat will have a simulated beach with simulated sunshine, sand, ocean. The works! And the crew members will spend a few days there after waking up so that their brains and bodies can completely recover, ready to fulfil their duties during the three months that they are awake.'

Craven turned to grin at the scanners. 'Well there you have it, seems like the folks down at Lifeboat Central have thought of everything!'

He turned his brilliant white smile back on his guests. 'Dr Goodwin, I'm sorry we didn't have time to ask about your area of expertise, maybe next time!' He leaned over and got very close to Rita. 'And thank you for coming on my program, Rita. I'd love to have you back, any time…'

The woman simpered, looking every inch the bimbo, while Craven gave her a suggestive smile; she was obviously a fan of his.

Dr Goodwin shuddered and looked away, mortified, as the broadcast ended.

6

Tom dozed drunkenly in a sun lounger, his Stetson pulled down low over his eyes and a large straw umbrella casting a shadow over his whole body.

'Hi, Tom.'

He grumbled and pushed his hat up an inch so that he could peek out from under it, squinting up with bloodshot eyes at the large figure standing over him. 'Barbara. Here to root around in my brain?'

'It's my job, I'm afraid. Are you going to give a pregnant woman a hard time about it?' Barbara smiled at him. As the group's psychiatrist it was her job to evaluate each of its members for any possible side-effects of the stasis or stress of the situation - purely a formality because the Lifeboat's design prevented any such occurrences and the crew were always kept well within the limits of human tolerance.

Tom glared up at her, but no matter how much belligerence he put into his expression, she still refused to go away. He considered rebelling and just walking away, but realised that it wasn't worth the bother; she would only come back again later and that bloody Adam thing would probably be with her. With a sigh he pushed his hat further back on his head and sat up, swivelling around on the lounger to face her. 'Of course not. Please, take a seat.'

'Thank you.' Barbara delicately sat down on the lounger next to his, groaning in pleasure as she took the weight off her feet.

Tom raised an eyebrow. 'You're only seven months pregnant, don't you think you're overdoing the whole suffering wife thing?'

'Of course I am, but Richard loves it; it makes him feel like he's needed.'

Tom snorted in amusement and the two of them glanced over at Richard, who was lying on a lounger about ten metres away, snoring gently in the shade of another umbrella.

Barbara looked at Tom critically, noting the dark circles under the bloodshot eyes. 'So, how are you feeling, Tom?'

'Fine, fine, quite hunky and even fairly dory in fact. A bit drunk, but you know how it is.'

'No ill effects from the stasis? Not seeing things? Didn't have any strange dreams last night? If I told you to hit yourself in the face would you do it?'

'Nope, nope, nope and nope. I am seeing double right now, but I'm fairly sure that's not from the stasis.'

'Hmm, no, I don't think that counts. Anything else?'

'I'm perfectly fine, Barbara. I wouldn't waste your time on me. If you want to psychoanalyse someone then maybe you should start with those three.' Tom pointed down at the water's edge where the three youngsters were rolling around in the sand and screeching in laughter.

Barbara shaded her eyes to look. 'What makes you say that? They're the healthiest people here, mentally. Is there something that makes you think that they aren't?'

'I suppose not, it's just that they're so damn cheerful all the time. It's disgusting. And it can't possibly be natural.' He said this with a bit of a grin on his face and Barbara returned it and shook her head wryly.

'There's nothing natural about this whole situation, Tom, that's why we have to look out for each other.' She patted him on the leg and struggled to her feet. 'Laying off the drink would probably do you some good, but apart from that you seem fine.'

'I'll take that under advisement.'

She waddled away, back to Richard.

As soon as her back was turned, Tom waved at the barmaid and she hurried over with another drink.

7

Tom tumbled dizzily, uncontrollably, plunging down a tunnel of stars that raced past, receding to a point far above him. An expanding blackness was fast coming up to meet him, a blackness in which nothing lived and nothing could live, threatening to swallow him. He tried to turn back, to get away from it, but there was another above, reaching down for him with dark tendrils which blotted out points of light that were whole suns and galaxies, snuffing them as if they were nothing. There was no escape to the sides either, because something equally malicious was lurking beyond the last remnants of light that flitted past. All he could do was drop endlessly, waiting for the dark to take him and he opened his mouth to rail against it, to deny its very existence, but...

...a hand shook him and he jerked awake with a start.

'Wha...?' Tom opened his eyes and blinked in the sudden light, his eyes watering, unable for a second to work out where, who, or even what he was.

The sun was half way to the horizon, the day more than three-quarters gone and he was still in his lounger, sprawled untidily with two of his limbs hanging off the edge. His hat had fallen off at some point and the shade of the umbrella no longer completely covered him, but it didn't matter; it wasn't possible for him to get burnt.

'Gah...' He covered his eyes with his hand to protect them, then squinted through the gaps between his fingers to look up at the girl who was standing above him. It was Tammy. 'Whaddya want?'

She loomed over him, hands on hips, topless, wearing only bikini bottoms and a smile. She was extremely cheerful in the face of his grumpy sleepiness. 'Hiya Tom! It's time for volleyball! Let's go!'

'Uhrrr, I really don't think so...'

Rachel now came running up, also topless and far too cheerful. 'Aw, come on, Tom! Barbara can't play this time and we need someone to even the numbers!'

Tammy grinned. 'Yeah, come on, Tom, you know you want to, really! Don't be such a square! And anyway, as the Health and Fitness supervisor, I'm ordering you to!'

Tom groaned, complaining and swearing under his breath, but struggled to stand nonetheless. He wavered on his feet and had to sit down again, the after-effects of the dream or whatever it had been, still with him, his head still spinning.

The two girls reached down, pulling him out of his chair by an arm each. 'Come on, old man!' They laughed and released him to run ahead of him.

Despite himself, Tom found the girls' enthusiasm somewhat contagious. 'There must be something in the water...' He followed them to the court at a more sedate pace, shaking his head and muttering to himself. 'And that's why I don't drink it.'

The rest of the group were already knocking the ball around and Barbara was sitting to one side, ready to referee.

They divided up into two teams, men against women, but with Adam replacing Barbara so that the teams remained even.

Tom always complained at being forced to join in, but he was actually a good player, much better than the rest, and enjoyed himself immensely every time they played. That day was no different and he was soon laughing with the rest as he sent the women diving and stumbling around trying to field his shots.

Barbara called a halt after an hour when the sun reached the horizon. Nobody wanted to stop, but she insisted, saying that she was hungry and there was a schedule to keep to, so eventually everybody agreed. They were all covered with sand, but they embraced anyway and at an unspoken agreement ran down to the sea as a group to wash it off. Barbara joined them and Richard folded her into his arms as they watched the others getting clean. Leo and the two girls were the most energetic; splashing and rubbing at each other, not at all shy about scrubbing sand off of even the most intimate parts of their lovers' bodies.

Tom found himself standing just to one side of the group. He still felt like a bit of an outsider, but each time they came out of stasis it got just a little bit better.

He noticed that Sarah and Elaine were looking at him with a speculative look on their faces. Caught up in the heat of the moment and the excitement of the game he smiled back at them.

Adam wandered over to him. 'Looks like you had some fun today after all.'

Some of Tom's good mood immediately fell away at the sight of Adam, but he grudgingly nodded.

Adam grinned at him. 'We've played this game many times now, you and I. When are you going to stop giving me such a hard time?'

'Things would get very boring, very quickly, if I let you have everything your own way, wouldn't it?'

Tom left Adam and sauntered over to join Elaine and Sarah. They smiled at him and together they walked over to the dining table that had been set up by the bar.

ARCHIVE C66

New Earth "Entertainment and Mental Health Research" facility.
15 years until launch.

A seventy year old man with messy white hair and small wire-rimmed glasses, dressed in a long white lab coat, stood behind a lab desk in front of a blackboard and addressed a group of men in grey suits. He looked like a stereotypical mad scientist from the twentieth and twenty-first centuries and it was fairly obvious that it was an image he cultivated; his glasses didn't have any lenses in them and besides, myopia was something that had been wiped out a very long time ago.

The desk was cluttered with scientific equipment, but it was all very dated. There were Bunsen burners, Tesla coils, various pieces of glassware containing bubbling liquids of all different colours and, bizarrely, a beach volleyball. He spoke English with a thick German accent, which was part of his persona.

Despite all the showmanship, the man, Professor Heinz, was a very respected scientist, although nobody quite knew why.

'Ya, ve found through various scientific studies zat ze best way of reducing stress and promoting ze group dynamic was by ze playing of ze *Beach Volleyball*.' He laughed and jumped up and down excitedly, waving his hands in glee. 'I am zo happy to be addink my expertise to ze Lifeboat project, my mutter is zo proud of me!'

He picked up the ball from the desk and hit it with his hand as if serving. He didn't do it very well and it shot off sideways, knocking over some glass test tubes which smashed on the floor. He didn't care though, and just smiled inanely at the men gathered around him.

8

The sun had completely gone by the time they sat down to dinner, but the table was softly lit by the full moon which was rising over the sea and the Tiki torches that had thrust into the sand around the table. The atmosphere was a lot more relaxed than it had been the previous day immediately after coming out of stasis; there was less of a focus on eating and more on socialising - the volleyball had done its job; raising pulses, getting the adrenaline flowing and banishing any remaining stiffness in both bodies and behaviour.

Tom sat between Sarah and Elaine as AHs served a dinner of seafood and salad and they laughed and talked together, eating food off of each other's plates and toasting each other with a light white wine.

Rachel, whose assigned job was that of nutritionist, kept an eye on everyone and made sure that they ate properly. When she spotted that Richard was not eating his vegetables she got up and told him off, jokingly spoon-feeding him. Barbara sat next to him through the whole thing, laughing and dabbing at the corner of his mouth with a napkin as if he were a baby. Richard sat and took it, amused and quite pleased to be the centre of attention for once, only a little bit ashamed.

After eating their fill they retired to the huts for the night.

Adam had been at the bar all evening and he remained where he was, silently watching them go.

Tom was about to go into his hut when Sarah and Elaine grabbed him by the hands and dragged him into theirs.

The three youths of course ended up together.

Richard and Barbara sat on the porch of their hut for a while, watching the stars come out in each other's arms. Their peace was disturbed when Leo, Rachel and Tammy came out of their hut, naked and laughing, and ran down to the sea. They weren't overly annoyed by the noise, but nonetheless stood up and went inside.

Four naked AHs, two men and two women, went into Jacob's hut and Adam smiled when he saw through his link that Jacob had them sit down and meditate with him before doing anything else.

John sat on his porch and read for a few hours before eventually retiring to bed. Adam was slightly worried about him; sex was such an important part of the human experience and aided the recovery from stasis to such an extent that it was an essential and irreplaceable part of the crew's activities.

He resolved to talk to Barbara about it the next day, see if she couldn't talk him into having some with an AH, or at least reading something a bit more pornographic than the classical literature that was his usual fare.

Just before midnight all became quiet and Adam froze in place, letting his mind sink into the ship's systems; there were a few things that needed his undivided attention.

9

Early the next morning, Tom wandered out of Sarah and Elaine's hut and stood, yawning and stretching, on the porch. He looked over his shoulder at the women; they were still sleeping, lying naked on the covers, arms around each other.

It had been a wonderfully fun night, but he was fairly sure that that was all that it was going to be: one night. Sarah and Elaine were in love with each other and it had been clear all along that he was there solely to provide them with for a bit of a change, an added stimulus. Perhaps they had even felt sorry for him. He didn't mind one bit, though; it had been very memorable and he had been extremely well taken care of.

He stepped down off the porch and walked the short distance to his own hut to have a shower before breakfast.

Adam watched from his place on the stool at the bar and smiled, pleased. After John, Tom was the one person in this group who least took advantage of the sexual activities available and it was especially good to see him voluntarily relating to others in the group.

He turned to make sure that everything was in its place and, of course, it was; the beach was spotless, the dining table had been removed, the barmaid was standing motionless in her place inside the bar hut and a buffet had been set up next to it.

The bar area slowly filled up as the crew came awake and started to want food. They took what they wanted from the buffet and sat on the sun loungers, eating informally, talking together, much more of a group, the separations much less in evidence. Even Tom took part in the conversation and looked like he was almost enjoying himself, although he did so with a whisky in his hand. It was his first, though; he hadn't downed any before leaving the bar area, and Adam hoped that meant he wasn't planning to drink as much as the day before.

While the crew had been sleeping the AHs had set up a complete medical suite on the sand of the beach beyond the volleyball court and Sarah now took up her doctor's duties and began to examine the group one by one, assisted by Elaine. The rest of the crew relaxed while they waited for their turn, swimming, reading, eating, drinking and talking.

In the late afternoon there was another volleyball match, this time with mixed teams, and Tom made sure to get himself on the same team as Sarah and Elaine. He did his best to impress and be friendly to them, but they only had eyes for each other and when the game finished they ignored him to wash each other off. He shrugged, grinning wryly to himself; he had apparently been right that the night before would be a one-off. It had been worth a shot though.

Adam provided further entertainment for them that evening by programing a spectacular sunset over the ocean, finished off by a meteor shower and the entire group sat close together on the sand to watch it. Jacob managed to persuade the three youngest members of the group to smoke a joint with him and for almost the first time since they had got to the beach there was quiet as Leo, Rachel and Tammy stared open-mouthed in wonder at the incredible colours of the artificially produced natural display in front of them and forgot to joke around.

Dinner was set out the same way as the night before, but it was less of a riotous feast and more of a comfortable meal between friends, with a bare minimum of joking around and much more conversation.

After dinner everyone split up into their groups and went their own way.

Tom watched Sara and Elaine leave hand in hand, disappearing into their hut and closing the door without sparing a glance for him, but he wasn't especially disappointed; he had an alternative already planned out. He went to his own hut and pressed a couple of icons on the computer screen attached to the wall. Minutes later the door opened and in walked two AHs, a male and a female. They smiled at him and he smiled back.

10

Breakfast the next day was the most informal yet, with everybody just eating wherever they felt like.

Adam stood by the bar wearing a differently patterned, but equally awful Hawaiian shirt with matching shorts and addressed them while they ate. 'Good morning everybody! As you know, unfortunately this is our last day here together. I hope you have all enjoyed yourselves!'

There were some groans at his pronouncement but he continued with a smile. 'I'm sure we would all like to thank Barbara, Rachel, Elaine and Sarah for taking such good care of us while we've been here. I know that some of you haven't made it particularly easy for them.'

Barbara called out. 'Don't worry Rachel, Richard knows he has to eat his vegetables from now on, or he won't get to play with my fine body!'

The group laughed at Richard's discomfort and Adam continued when they settled down again. 'Yes, well, have fun today because I'm sorry, but from tomorrow the rest of you will have to start doing some work.' Adam smiled and nodded, then without any further comment he walked away and out of the Beach Room.

The group's mood had been somewhat spoiled and they continued to eat in silence for a while until Jacob chuckled. 'Whoa, what a downer!'

'Yes. He could at least have waited until we'd finished eating.' John dropped a half-finished slice of melon back on his plate with a grimace and pushed it away.

'Don't mind him, it's just his programming,' said Barbara.

Tom was curious. 'Have you ever tried to shrink an Artificial Human?'

Barbara snorted. 'Who do you think I am? Freud? I have the same amount of training in my job as all of you do. Five years intensive cramming isn't enough to be able to get into the mind of one of those.'

Richard reached out and hugged her to him. 'I'm really not sure there'd be a lot to root around in if you did try. I think it would be more Leo's field of expertise.'

Leo held his hands up in protest. 'Don't look at me, I'm no better off than Barbara, I can just about handle the ship's computers and all they do is drive us around, Adam walks and talks...'

'And fucks!' Tammy broke in with a huge grin.

'Oh, YEAH!' said Rachel with a wide-eyed grin of her own and the group laughed.

Leo got them back on track. 'Anyway, he's a whole other order of complexity and I wouldn't know where to even start with his programming. I'm not sure that there is anyone alive now who would know the first thing about building or configuring an AH, let alone one with AI.'

Tom sighed. 'Yeah, machines building machines that build Artificial Humans that take care of real humans, who build machines that build machines...'

Jacob nodded, wide-eyed, spellbound with the possibilities. 'Far out, man...'

Tom turned to him. 'And what about you, Jacob, if our engines suddenly stopped working, could you get us going again, or are we all going to have to get out and push?'

'No, man, me and engines go way back, we have an understanding, you know?' Jacob was one of the few members of the entire crew of the Lifeboat who had actually been involved with the Lifeboat project prior to launch, joining the engineering teams responsible for their design and construction as a young man.

'Hey! Old people! Are we going to sit around boring each other senseless or are we going to do something fun with our last day here? I'm going for a swim, who's coming?' Tammy stood up and stripped down to her bikini. Without waiting for an answer she ran to the water and dived straight in.

Jacob took one last drag on his spliff before putting it out and placing it carefully to one side for later. 'Our health and fitness expert has a point, man.' He stood up and took off his shirt and shorts, revealing a very small red thong. He strolled down to the water where Tammy was waiting for them.

The group watched him go, amused, then, as one, they stood, took their clothes off and went to join them.

ARCHIVE D14234

Security feed. Executive viewing room One Alpha. New Earth orbital yard. 5 years until launch.

A group of people stood looking out of a viewing window in an orbital shipyard.

Among the group was Dr Adam Goodwin. He had deteriorated considerably, becoming an old man in the last few years, with sparse wispy white hair and liver spots. He looked very frail and was confined to a wheelchair; the stresses of the project had affected him, ageing him much more than was normal for a human race who had long ago perfected ways of delaying the process. He wore his white lab-coat, still stubbornly involved in the project despite his poor health.

Most of the rest of the group, men and women both, were dressed in light grey suits, but there were a couple of darker grey suits scattered among them. However, no matter their rank, every last one of them had an air of importance, or at least self-importance about them.

Beyond the window was a Lifeboat in the final stages of construction. It was illuminated a bright white that contrasted sharply with the blackness of space behind it and the dark grey polymer of the scaffolding that surrounded it. As they watched, the registration number was being written near the nose in black, block figures. The numbers and letters were made small by perspective, but they were in fact huge, each the size of a fifty-storey hab-block.

One middle-aged man with ginger hair and freckles stood out from the rest of the group, looking less than comfortable in his dark blue suit, as if he wasn't used to wearing one. He kept putting his finger in the collar of his shirt, pulling it away from his neck and grimacing. 'That's a hell of a lot of paint…'

'It's not paint, Mr President,' the weak and breathy voice of Dr Goodwin answered him. 'It's a special treatment that changes the reflective properties of the polymer that comprises the protective outer skin of the Lifeboat and makes it appear any colour we want. We can't use paint because it would be stripped off almost instantly once the ship started accelerating.'

'Ah. That makes sense, I suppose.' The President stopped fiddling with his tie for a second and leaned in closer to the window. 'It really doesn't look big enough for four million people. How the hell is this ever going to work, Doctor?'

'We've run the numbers over and over, Mr President, and it will work trust me.' Dr Goodwin grimaced and shifted uncomfortably in his wheelchair as he answered; he wasn't entirely happy with the whole project, even though it was supposed to be his "baby" - he had serious doubts about the viability of the whole idea of sending out Lifeboats and, even though he tried not to let them show, they did.

He was absolutely positive that if they had just given him a team and let him spend some time searching, even a few years, then they could have found a much more elegant and efficient solution to the problem, one that had a higher possibility of success, but the powers that be had jumped on the Lifeboat project as soon as he'd proposed it and after that nobody had wanted to know about anything else. He had lobbied for continuing research anyway, but the Lifeboats had been too glamorous, too romantic and had seemed to take on a life of its own, starting a media frenzy that left no room for alternatives, In the end all he could do was try to do the best job that he could with it, especially seeing as there wasn't going to be a backup plan.

He turned his wheelchair to face the President and drew breath to make the speech that he had given every two years in that very same room to the previous twenty-six newly appointed heads of state after they had asked the same question or something very similar.

'With a cargo of 4 million people the only way for power levels to remain at maximum over a journey lasting billions of years is to keep the vast majority of them in stasis. Groups of ten will be awakened for three months at a time so as to avoid so called "stasis psychosis". These groups will typically consist of five men and five women, conserving families and relationships wherever possible, with at least one crew member from each group having a minimum of training in some part of running and maintaining the ship, such as computing, engineering, stasis field theory, nutrition, mental health and so on. They'll have these "jobs" purely for morale purposes, of course; the A.I's and A.H's will be perfectly capable of running the ship without them.'

'Ten people? That's hardly enough for a decent game of beach volleyball! And only three months? Why so short?'

'Any longer than that and the time between Recovery periods goes up for everyone, which would also increase the risk of psychosis. And we have calculated that ten is the maximum safe number of people that can be awake at a time without risking using resources faster than they can be regenerated. Anyway, the hundred-thousand-year-long stasis period will pass in an instant for the people on board.'

The man shrugged. 'I guess... I suppose it could be worse.'

'Yes, Mr President, very much worse. In addition to the normal crew members, each ship will, wherever possible, have one Astrophysicist, selected from the present community of experts in their field. That person's job will be to prepare a report on awakening to inform the rest of the passengers of the current status of the Universe in layman's terms. On paper they will be there to give warning of any possible obstacles along the course of each Lifeboat and later help to identify stars that will likely develop habitable planets after the next big bang. That is already going to be handled more than efficiently by the A.I. though, so obviously this is once again just for morale purposes; like the rest of the passengers they are not actually needed in the slightest. In fact, if it wasn't for the risk of losing precious genetic stock to stasis psychosis we wouldn't actually need to bother waking the cargo at all.'

'Now if you'll follow my assistant, Mr President, we'll show you how the Executive Lifeboat is progressing.'

Dr Goodwin waited until the group had followed his assistant from the room, then moved his wheelchair up as close to the window as he could get and stared out at the Lifeboat.

As a last ditch effort for the survival of humanity it disappointed him, even though it had been his idea. It was inelegant, inefficient, and so much of humanity would be left behind to die, albeit in billions of years. There was no guarantee that the human race would last that long anyway; there was always the possibility of someone doing something stupid and wiping the whole lot of them out, but it was the best he had been allowed to come up with. He just hoped that others would work on more plausible solutions in the future - they had plenty of time after all.

He was also *extremely* glad that he wouldn't live long enough to be packed like a frozen fish onto one of his creations.

11

Adam returned to the beach just in time for the daily volleyball game and announced that everything was ready for them to resume their shipboard lives. The match and the dinner that followed were therefore somewhat more subdued than previous days as the time when the group had to leave the beach behind swiftly approached, casting a shadow over the activities.

While remains of the meal were cleared away by AHs the crew drifted across to the bar area. Richard and Barbara sat together on the sand looking out at the sea. Tammy, Rachel and Leo went down to the water and began splashing naked in the shallows, laughing, eking out the last moments of playtime, just out of the reach of the light from the Tiki torches but still in full view of the others in the illumination provided by the full moon. The rest sat on the loungers to engage in quiet conversation.

Tom sat with a last whisky in his hand, talking with John.

John was the group's historian and Tom always enjoyed conversations with him. That night the man had some particularly interesting observations to make about human evolution, or the lack of it.

'Mankind has only survived this long precisely *because* of its stagnation. The most difficult periods in history, the most destructive setbacks, have always been due to over-ambition or over-reaching. From the wars of old Earth, to the "Colonisation Conflicts", to the mass suicides of "The Acceptance". Each of those threatened to snuff out the light of human existence once and for all. It wasn't until we realised that there just wasn't any sense in striving for more, that we already knew everything and we needed for nothing, that we became safe. We could simply *live*. However we wanted to.'

Tom nodded. 'And it has taken an extinction event of this magnitude to bring us out of our stupor.'

'Even so, it hasn't really changed anything. The technology used to build this ship existed for millions of years before we decided to use it - we could have made this journey any time we wanted.'

'Do you think the people we left behind will keep working on the problem?'

'I shouldn't think so for one second.'

'You don't believe that someone will come up with a better idea? Apparently Dr Goodwin was always sure that there was a more "elegant" solution, as he put it in his diaries.'

John shook his head. 'But he never came up with one.'

'I don't think they let him try.'

John laughed so harshly, it was almost a bark. 'Because everyone was already quite comfortable with his original plan; it was familiar to them and they didn't want anything new or different. Plus ça change, plus c'est la même chose. Nothing changes. Look around you, life continues.'

'Not quite,' Tom indicated the group down by the water's edge. 'It looks like there's trouble in paradise.'

Tammy was crying and shouting something incoherent at Leo and Rachel. Leo reached out, trying to grab hold of her, but she pushed him away forcefully and stumbled up the beach.

They watched as she ran past them. Tears were streaming down her face but her expression was more one of fury than anything else. 'Door!'

The door appeared at her angrily shouted command and she raced through it. It closed behind her and disappeared again, cutting off her enraged sobs.

Leo and Rachel came slowly up the beach, hand in hand, shocked and more than a little upset. They collected their clothes and Tammy's and started to get dressed.

Barbara had watched the whole thing and she now stood up and went over to them. 'Are you guys OK? What happened?'

Leo blinked and looked at her. He seemed almost in shock. 'I have no idea. One minute we were just talking and the next she was screaming at us for leaving her out of things.'

'Which is completely unfair! We do everything together!' Rachel did her best to wipe away her tears but they kept coming back.

Leo pulled her into a hug. 'I think she's just tired. We've been having some late nights…'

Barbara nodded. 'I'll have a talk with her later and make sure she's OK, but I'm sure you're right. Just try to get some more sleep, OK? I know that you're young and you want to have fun, but remember we all have jobs to do and there are a lot of people depending on us - it can't all be fun and games!' She grinned at them and they looked sheepish as they hesitantly smiled back.

Adam came over from where he had been talking to Richard and addressed the group. 'It's time to start winding things down here I'm afraid. If anybody wants to go for a last swim please be my guest, but I declare "R and R" officially over. Thank you for coming and I hope to see you all here once more in 3 months or 100,000 years, whichever comes last!'

The group dutifully laughed at Adam's joke.

The door appeared again and remained opened - a not too subtle invitation to leave and get back to what served as their normal lives.

Sarah and Elaine walked hand in hand down to the water and waded in for a last paddle, embracing while they looked up at the stars, but Richard took Barbara around the waist and led her out into the white corridor beyond the door. They were followed by everyone else except for Tom who remained on his lounger, sipping his drink with a thoughtful expression on his face.

12

The darkness beckoned as Tom fell, and fell, and fell…

13

Tom wandered into breakfast the next day to find that most people were already there. He yawned as he got food from the buffet then shuffled across the room, almost sleepwalking, to his place at the table. He really hadn't slept well; he kept having the same dream over and over and it woke him with a start every few hours. He was fairly sure that it was just his work weighing on his mind, though; it was a heavy responsibility knowing that the fate of the whole ship was in his hands and he'd be fine once he got to it and could make sure that they had a safe course plotted.

As he crossed the room, Tom noticed that Adam was having a serious conversation with Barbara and Sarah and he assumed that it was about Tammy. He tried to listen in, but they finished just as he was arriving and he couldn't catch any of it so he just sat down and began to eat, munching unenthusiastically on some cereals.

Adam watched Tom curiously from his place at the head of the table. 'Tired, Tom?'

Barbara looked up when she heard Adam and her eyes widened. 'Wow, you look like shit, Tom!'

'Thank you, Barbara, that training of yours has really taught you the best things to say to perk me up.'

'My pleasure.'

Adam cut in. 'The beach was supposed to be a chance to rest.'

'I rested fine, thanks.'

Sarah interjected. 'Maybe you should drink a bit less alcohol next time; we're none of us as young as we used to be.'

Tom laughed. 'Nonsense, I feel a billion years young!' He was going to say more but stopped and looked up as Leo and Rachel came in, supporting Tammy between them. All three looked exhausted and somewhat listless, but Tammy was smiling, albeit not quite as enthusiastic as usual. They filled plates then sat down with the others at the table.

Once everyone was in their place Adam stood up and smiled, meeting their eyes one at a time as he spoke. 'Good morning, everybody. I trust that you are all feeling at least a little bit rested after your days on the beach? Even if some of you did overdo it somewhat! First of all, just so that you know, Tammy is perfectly fine, she's just a bit tired and there is nothing to worry about. Barbara and Sarah will re-evaluate her later today and keep an eye on her for a while, but they don't see any reason why she shouldn't be up and about. As for the rest of us, it's time to take on our appointed tasks. As soon as we get them over and done with, the sooner we can get back to enjoying ourselves!'

'Hear, hear!' Jacob raised his glass of juice in approval.

The group laughed and went back to eating as Adam sat down and quiet conversation started back up.

As Tom ate, he watched Adam - he was keeping an eye on Tammy as unobtrusively as possible, trying to make it seem as if he wasn't.

There was undoubtedly more going on than Adam was telling them, but he had no idea what that could possibly be. Not yet anyway.

14

Tom's laboratory on board the ship was actually just a multipurpose room that could be used for anything and there were no scientific instruments, no computers or desks to be seen, it was only a bare white room like any other; there was no point in having a dedicated astrophysics lab on board when the only astrophysicist in the crew was awake for just 3 months every one hundred thousand years.

As soon as Tom walked in he called up the latest representation of the observed universe and walked around the hologram with a tablet in his hands, making notes occasionally but mostly just getting a feel for it, looking for the differences between it and the one he remembered from three months and so long ago. He inspected it from every angle, turning it round and expanding it where necessary to look at whatever caught his attention.

He liked to take a look at the overall state of the universe itself before searching out the dangers that might be lurking in wait on their projected course; it gave him a better picture of what was happening in general and helped him to predict possible variations in the behaviour of different objects as the universe collapsed. So many massive bodies getting closer together did funny things to the universe, not just to physical effects like gravity but also to space-time itself; there were many very real dangers that couldn't be seen and needed to be felt out, almost intuitively. Besides, he was an astrophysicist, not a navigator and this was what he had signed up for: the chance to study the universe collapse in on itself. The second biggest show that there had ever been.

The hours passed in a blur and he would have been there for many more if he hadn't been interrupted by the chime for lunch. He almost didn't believe that so much time had passed until his stomach growled and he realised how hungry he was.

He ate lunch as quickly as he could, poring over the notes he had made on the tablet, taking no part in the conversation and barely making eye contact with anyone, then, as soon as he could, he excused himself from the table and hurried back to his lab.

He knew that he could very easily spend the rest of his day, if not the rest of his life, doing only he'd been doing that morning, but he summoned all of his willpower and forced himself to progress with his work, promising himself, as always, that he would return to the fun stuff once his work was done. Not that the rest of his work wasn't interesting as well, of course.

He called up the representation again, but this time he had the computer plot the positions of the Lifeboats as well and began looking at the red icons, representing lost Lifeboats.

This wasn't strictly part of his job, but he felt that there was something to learn from the mistakes that other people made and also he felt that someone should take the time to bear witness to the end of so many human beings. There were only a handful of red icons so far, thankfully, and each was a tragedy, but even so the computer told him that the losses were well within the acceptable margins that some nitwit in an office had set out at the beginning of the mission, at least when taken in terms of the immense number of Lifeboats scattered about the map, expanding like a cloud of gas.

He focussed on one of the red dots and moved the representation back in time a few thousand years, zooming in to see how the Lifeboat had tried to squeeze through the gap between two galaxies in mid-collision and had failed. It was an unfortunate reality that in their race for the edge of the Universe some risks had to be taken and, instead of going millions of years out of their way, the crew of that Lifeboat had tried to outrun the collision before it happened. It looked like they had almost made it but they had been slowed down at the last moment by a black hole that hadn't appeared on their scanners until it was too late - black holes were pesky like that sometimes.

He was sure that the Adam aboard had weighed the risks and rewards carefully, with the help of the astrophysicist, if they had one, but even so it angered him that the A.I. had agreed to gamble with so many human lives.

He zoomed back out and waded in amongst the stars. He went to the golden symbol representing his own Lifeboat and followed the golden line indicating the route that they had taken to get to their present position, noting the objects that they had passed since he had last been awake and seeing that his predictions had been correct. Then he started walking along the path he had projected the last time he had been awake, seeing if anything had cropped up that needed urgent attention, something that had been previously obscured and had appeared on the scanners, like the black hole that had caused the downfall of the other Lifeboat.

The Lifeboat resembled less the sailing ships and aircraft of old and more a projectile, fired into the unknown, and at the speed they were going course corrections had to be made thousands or even millions of years in advance. That meant he couldn't just look at what they would pass in the next hundred thousand years, he had to look as far into the future as he could and, if at all possible, plot a course for the Lifeboat that took them all the way to the edge of the observed universe. Undoubtedly, the computer could do the job much quicker than he could and he usually took a look at its suggestions, but, as humanity had found out the hard way, computers, and even AI's, weren't infallible.

Tom frowned as he noticed an anomaly close to the golden line as it curved through a particularly densely populated part of space about two million ship years ahead - there was something emerging from behind an immense absorption nebula. He zoomed in on it and walked around it, trying to find a better angle, but there wasn't one; the ship was rendering it as just an indistinct glow, meaning it still didn't know exactly what it was, but it was predicting that it would pass within a few hundred light years of their path. That would be fine if the object turned out to be something innocuous and boring, like a galaxy, but if the bright smear turned out to be the edge of an accretion disk around one of the ultramassive black holes that had been forming recently, which were magnitudes greater in size than supermassive black holes, then it would warp gravity to such an extent that it would require careful navigating of what would be troubled space around it. It might even warrant scrapping his entire course and plotting a new one to give it a wide berth.

He would have to consider very carefully before making his choice; they were already on the most optimal course he had been able to find, any other might delay them for hundreds of thousands of years, so if he decided to divert and the blur turned out to be nothing then he would be reducing their chances of survival for no reason. However, if he did decide to chance it and it turned out to be life threatening...

Adam shook his head and smiled wryly; now he knew how the astrophysicist on that Lifeboat must have felt.

It was a big decision, one he needed a clear head and a lot of time to make, but the day was fast drawing to a close, so he decided to leave it for the morning.

The tablet recorded his notes as he spoke them. 'Astrophysics report. Current Situation. In the last hundred thousand years, ship relative, our course has deviated only slightly from the charted in order to avoid a Dark Matter cloud and the remnants of a supernova. Projected course is clear for at least two million years ship time, but has possible problems to be resolved that may require a drastic course change before then. The situation is being studied. End report.'

Tom turned to leave, but halted in his tracks when he caught sight of something out of the corner of his eye - the model was supposed to be stationary, inert, but the brilliant white ball at its heart seemed to be pulsing with a life of its own. Rationally he knew that was impossible, but he couldn't help himself and he hesitantly reached out to pull at it, expanding it.

The gentle green glow cast by the cloud of Lifeboats passed beyond the walls and the room turned a pure, brilliant white as the centre of the universe filled the room, so bright that Tom had to squint against it, until he thought to dim it.

The closer to the centre he got, the more chaotic things were, the more distorted, but he was able to make out some individual features; galaxies were colliding five or six or more at a time, black holes were draining the energy from whatever they came across, clouds of super-hot gasses were everywhere and there, at the very centre…

Tom expanded the object and the room dimmed as most of the light sources disappeared through the walls. The details of what lie in the middle of the mayhem were hazy because of the sheer number of objects that surrounded it, but the computer had put together its best guess; a composite drawn in real time from the data shared by the scanners of all of the Lifeboats - one of the true advantages of instantaneous communication.

An immense mass of black sat at the centre of the Universe, slowly drawing in all the matter around it, tearing apart existence and destroying time itself.

Tom stared at it, feeling himself being drawn into the darkness. This was what he had dreamt about, this was what had kept him awake for hours last night and then woken him again when he finally drifted off in exhaustion. Despite the fact that it was only a holographic image he could feel its pull, could feel it calling to him, feel it tugging at his soul…

'Tom!'

Slowly, Tom dragged his eyes away from the hole. He blinked and rubbed his eyes before looking towards the source of the voice.

Adam stood in the doorway.

Tom punched a button on the tablet and the lights came on as the 3D representation disappeared.

'Hi, Tom. Everything alright? Find anything out of the ordinary?'

Tom slowly came back to himself. 'No… er, nothing. Why? Should I have?'

If anything Adam's smile widened more. 'Of course not! But you were so absorbed in your work that I had to call you three times. I thought you'd found something.'

'No, nothing. I was just daydreaming. I'm almost done here.'

There was an awkward silence while Adam smiled at Tom, as if waiting for him to say something more, unnaturally holding his smile well beyond the time when a human would have had to let it drop. Eventually the AI chuckled. 'Well then.'

'Yes?' Tom raised an eyebrow.

Without another word Adam turned in place and walked back out of the room, leaving Tom staring after him, mystified.

15

Tom spun, weightless, unable to control himself, falling down the tunnel of light that wasn't as bright as it had been as more of the matter, the *life* passing him was swallowed.

The blackness above was getting closer and closer in its quest to meet up with the darkness that was lying in wait below and he wasn't sure which one of them terrified him more.

'Tom!'

He was woken by a hand shaking him by the shoulder and for the second time in a few days he came out of the dream and found himself looking up at Tammy. She was wearing only slightly more clothing than she had at the beach, a halter top and small panties, and she looked very concerned for him.

'Are you alright?'

'What?'

'I could hear you shouting from the corridor and I thought you were in trouble. That was some kind of dream you were having!'

Tom sat up in bed and rubbed his eyes. When he opened them again Tammy was still watching him. 'Yeah, I'm fine, thanks.'

She sat down on the bed next to his feet. 'Do you want to talk about it?'

'Not really...' He hesitated. 'I've been having this dream the last few days... it's nothing, it's just got into my head. What about you, are you alright now?'

'Yeah, I'm fine. I sat down with Barbara and we had a bit of a chat.'

'That's always fun.'

Tammy smiled wryly. 'Yeah, I don't believe in all that stuff normally, but I think I needed it this time; I needed to hear her say I'd be OK. I've been feeling a bit off the last few days, like I've got a shorter temper or something.'

'You're not pregnant or having your period, are you?'

Tammy hit him on the leg, hard, but smiled. 'You men! Always thinking that we're only ever irrational because of "women's problems."'

'Sorry.'

She laughed. 'Don't worry, that's the first thing that Barbara asked me as well! And no, I'm not either of those things.'

'Good, I'm not sure that I could handle a hysterical woman at this time of night.'

She hit him again and they laughed.

'So, why are you up and about so late?'

'I was hungry and was going to get some food. I couldn't sleep; I'm not used to sleeping on my own.'

'Why were you on your own? What about Leo and Rachel?'

'I've decided to take a bit of a break. Try and get some rest. Doctor's orders!' She grinned. 'It's not working very well so far!'

Tom smiled cheekily. 'You don't have to be on your own, you know; there are plenty of other options.'

Tammy smiled back. 'Yeah, I know… John's probably still awake and reading in the common room…'

Tom laughed. 'Why go all the way to the common room? Why don't you just get in bed with me?' He winked then looked her up and down exaggeratedly; she was an extremely good-looking young woman, but he was only really joking, he wouldn't ever expect her to take him up on it.

'OK!' There wasn't even the slightest hesitation before she answered and she stood up, stripping off her clothes before slipping into bed beside him.

Tom's look of surprise lasted only a couple of seconds until Tammy's lips fastened onto his and then he just gave in and kissed her back just as enthusiastically, the dream completely forgotten.

ARCHIVE D978

Humanity-wide Retinal Broadcast from the President's office, New Earth. Three years until launch.

A young woman in a dark blue suit stood in the president's office on New Earth. Black cloth liberally draped the office and covered the desk behind her.

She stood in silence for a good few seconds, solemnly composing herself, and the entire human race watched her, waiting to hear the announcement that was so important that it had been broadcast to their retinas without prior warning.

Quadrillions held their breath; this close to Launch it wasn't likely to be good news.

'Hello, everybody, I apologise for interrupting your day, but I have some bad news, I'm afraid. I've just been informed that Doctor Adam Goodwin, has passed away quietly in his home. The "saviour of mankind" and "father of the Lifeboat project" has not lived to see his dream brought to fruition. For the first time in history we are proclaiming a civilisation-wide day of mourning. Permission to hold a memorial service is given to any and all who wish to do so. For now, please join me in a moment of silence while we give thanks for a great man whose life was well spent.'

She bowed her head and the human race followed her lead.

16

While he sometimes enjoyed the ministrations of the AHs, Tom felt that their programmed responses and unlimited energy made the experience more akin to masturbation than to sex and he much preferred the touch of a real person.

Tammy responded to his every desire with an eagerness that delighted him. There was an enthusiasm, a youth and an energy about her that wasn't nearly the same as the cold efficiency of the AHs, although there were times when Tom thought that he detected a hint of desperation about her lovemaking, as if she was trying to forget something, or run from something.

After hours of intense exertions with her, he was so exhausted that he fell asleep without any problem.

The dream didn't revisit Tom that night.

When he woke up the next morning she had gone. He swivelled round and sat on the side of the bed, rubbing his eyes. He smiled, stood up and padded naked into the bathroom for a shower.

When he was clean and dressed he left the room and made his way to breakfast. Tammy came out of her own room at the same time and they walked together towards the common room.

'I missed you this morning.'

Tammy smiled up at him. 'I woke up early. You were sleeping so well I didn't want to wake you.'

'Thank you for last night.'

'You're welcome, I really enjoyed myself. It's funny, I don't know what happened; I heard you calling out and only wanted to see if you were alright, but then… I don't know what came over me!'

'I'm glad you stayed. I had a lot of fun, I hope you're ok about it.'

'Yeah, I'm fine, and I had a lot of fun too! But I've kinda decided to go back to the guys, you know? Maybe I was just a bit annoyed with them and needed some comfort or something. I dunno. Whatever it was, I'm over it, thanks to you! But I love them, so I need to sort things out with them.'

They stopped at the door to the dining room and Tom smiled at her. 'Well, thank you again for a wonderful night.'

'My pleasure, Tom, I hope you sleep better from now on.'

'Thanks.'

She turned and went in.

Tom watched Tammy walking away, savouring the memories of a wonderful night, then followed her.

17

Barbara, Elaine, Sarah and Tom were on their mid-afternoon break, relaxing in the sofa area of the common room, eating the snacks that were set out for them by the AHs every day at this time and taking advantage of Tammy's absence to talk about her case.

'So, what do you think caused her outburst, Barbara?' Tom asked. 'I would have thought she'd have been more likely to have an episode like that at the start of R and R, not at the end. I mean, yes, we were all disappointed to be leaving, but we were all pretty relaxed... Not as relaxed as Jacob obviously...'

They laughed gently at his joke before Barbara answered. 'I'm fairly sure it was a product of the relationship they're in; they're young, they're immature... She more than likely got jealous over nothing.'

'I think you're right.' Sarah agreed. 'I couldn't find anything physically wrong with her. A few of her numbers were a bit off, though, but that could have meant anything - from a having had a bad night to, I don't know, a migraine at the worst. I wanted to check the records of the other Stasis Groups, to see if anybody else had had similar results and whether anything had happened to them, but Adam wouldn't let me.'

Elaine interjected. 'Yeah, that was a bit weird, wasn't it?'

Tom looked at her. 'What was?'

'Well, when Sarah asked Adam for the records he went quiet for a second in that creepy way the AHs have when they have nothing to do. He came out of it pretty quickly, though, and told us we couldn't have the records because of patient confidentiality, then just smiled at us and walked away.'

Sarah shrugged. 'I can understand that up to a point, but I wasn't asking for anyone's records in particular, just general information on whether there had been any similar incidents in any of the other groups.'

While Sarah had been speaking Leo had entered the room. He grabbed a drink and some snacks and came over to the group, sitting on the arm of the sofa that Sarah and Elaine were sharing.

Tom looked thoughtful. 'Adam was a bit weird with me earlier on as well. He came into my lab and asked me if I'd found anything unusual. It was almost as if he was expecting me to find something bad and was checking to see whether I had.'

Leo had been listening idly, but now he broke in, albeit a bit hesitantly. 'Hey, Doc, uh, do you think… I mean, is weirdness contagious?'

Sarah laughed. 'No, Leo, not as far as I know.'

'Well, I wasn't going to say anything because I thought it was a one-off, but, hearing you guys talk… It might not be related, but the computers are acting a bit funny as well.'

Tom's eyes narrowed as he looked at Leo. 'In what way?'

'Well, when I was training for this they told me the computers had been specifically designed to be as simple as possible so that they could do the same job over and over for billions and billions of years without ever making any mistakes, right? But, get this, there have been little errors cropping up everywhere, errors that I wouldn't expect to see cropping up this quickly even in a normal computer, let alone on a ship that's supposed to last forever and be the ultimate in human technology. I don't know if it's a design fault or what, but I kinda hope it isn't 'cos it means we'd be totally fucked way before we even reach the edge of the universe!'

The group received the news in shocked silence.

Tom threw the remains of his snack on the table, leaving it for the AHs to clear up, then stood up and looked around the group. 'So, we've got medical issues, Adam is acting funny, and now the computers are on the fritz… I think I should go and have a little chat with Jacob, I really fucking hope there's nothing wrong with the engines.'

He walked away and behind him the conversation immediately turned to more trivial matters in that way that modern humanity had of pushing aside anything that was difficult or important and leaving it for someone else to sort out.

'God! This pregnancy is killing me! Do you think I can get a massage sometime, Sarah? Elaine? Don't get me wrong, Richard does his best, but you can't beat a woman's touch!'

The group was laughing as the door closed behind Tom, cutting them off.

18

The Stasis Room Storage Bay, *SRSB*, by necessity occupied the vast majority of the space on the ship.

When he had first explained the idea behind his ship's design to the committee responsible for the project, Dr Adam Goodwin had likened the Lifeboats to icebergs, saying that the SRSB was analogous to the 90% of an iceberg that was under the water. Most people would never see it and weren't even really aware that it was there, but it was the most important part of it, without which the whole thing would sink without trace.

Tom entered the bay through a short corridor that led to a small balcony looking out over the cavernous space. The balcony was lined with railings on both sides for safety but, surprisingly, not straight ahead in front of the entrance.

He had only ever been here once before, back before the launch of the ship, and again he marvelled at the sheer size of the thing. Just like the submerged part of the iceberg that Dr Goodwin had talked about, it was something that you would never suspect even existed if you confined yourself exclusively to the comparatively cramped space at the nose of the immense cone that was the Lifeboat, which was what the vast majority of its passengers did.

He went to the railing on the left of the opening and grabbed a tight hold when a sudden wave of vertigo threatened to overcome him; his brain tried to convince him that down was in a different direction to the one his feet were insisting on. He bent over the rail, careful not to put too much weight on it - despite the fact that it was made of the same material as the structure of the ship itself and was more durable than diamond - and looked down at the white roof of his own stasis pod, about ten metres below him. It was sitting flush up against the wall of the nose section from where he had just come, the number 82,458 stencilled on it in large black writing. He concentrated on the number, using it to ground himself, then, once he'd regained a modicum of control, he lifted his eyes to look up at the rest of the space, or at least as much as could be seen in the low light.

Thousands upon thousands of white cubes, stasis pods, were stacked from floor to ceiling in every direction in concentric rings, gathered around a central axis, a tunnel that had been left clear of obstructions, enough space for a stasis pod to pass to and from its place and for the engineer to travel to his engine room at the back of the ship.

Tom moved in front of the gap in the railings, took a deep breath, then stepped forward into thin air.

A golden lattice field came into being around him, completely enclosing him and as soon as it had him firmly in its grip it accelerated forward, racing into the gap between the stasis rooms.

The lattice cage flew along the tunnel, past ring after ring of pods, separated by a pod-sized gap, that were illuminated only by the gentle golden light of the cage. On his previous visit Tom had thought that it looked very much like he was flying through a cob of sweetcorn, but today it reminded him uncomfortably of the dream that had been plaguing him recently and he shuddered and closed his eyes, shutting out the sight before he was overcome by the fears the dream brought with it. His anxiety was only made worse by the oppressive silence, though, which in turn was exacerbated by the knowledge that there about four million people around him, slumbering in dreamless sleep, trusting him to do his job and make sure that the path ahead of them was safe.

Thankfully the journey was short - the SRSB was more than ten kilometres in length, but the journey took just over twenty seconds - and very soon he became aware of the light of his destination in the distance. In a rush the lattice cage docked with a balcony that was in every way identical to the one that he had just stepped off of, except that it didn't have a stasis pod docked below it.

The cage receded from around him and he stepped forward and walked down a short corridor, the gently audible hum of the engines already pervading the space around him.

19

The engine room was another immense space, not quite as big as the SRSB, but certainly far larger than any of the rooms at the front of the ship in the residential areas, taking up as it did the entirety of the final half-kilometre of the base of the cone that was the Lifeboat.

The first thing that anybody saw on coming down the corridor, and the only thing that could be seen until they reached the engine room itself because it completely blocked the view, was the huge screen. It was free standing about ten metres from the entrance, at least fifty metres wide by twenty tall and set in the middle of a white platform. The platform ended in mid-air, without even the safety of railings, and there was a large gap (a sheer drop all the way to the "base" of the Lifeboat, along the length of which were located the gravity generators) beyond which Tom could just about make out the immense shapes of the engines themselves. To Tom the engines were just a mess of pipes, metal and incomprehensible glowing features, but they were like children to Jacob. Their hum was more than merely audible here; it was a vibration that permeated Tom's bones and made his skin crawl and itch and he wondered how Jacob could stand it for hours on end.

The screen usually showed information on the state of the hundreds of engines and shipwide energy stores, but when Tom entered it was dark, inactive, and Jacob was sitting cross legged in front of it with his eyes closed.

Tom walked over and stood in front of him. He waited a few seconds for Jacob to acknowledge his presence in some way, but he didn't move or even seem to realise Tom was there. 'Um, Jacob?'

Jacob slowly opened his eyes to look up at Tom and smiled broadly. 'Oh, hey man! Haven't seen you down here before! Do you want the guided tour?'

Tom eyed the sheer drop, more than ten metres away, but far too close for his liking. 'Maybe later, thanks.'

'Sure, man, sure, that's cool! Any time! So what can I do for you, then?'

'I wanted to know if you'd had time to run any diagnostics yet.'

'Yes, and no.'

Tom blinked, 'I'm sorry?'

Jacob grinned. 'Yes, I've run the diagnostics through the computer and they tell the same story as ever, that everything is all cool and groovy and blah, blah, blah, but no, I haven't had time to do my own diagnostics.'

'Your own diagnostics?'

'Yeah, *my* diagnostics. The engines talk to me, man, they tell me how they are, and I trust *that* more than I trust any damn computer. Anyway, that's what I was doing when you came in - listening to what they have to say and right now they're purring like kittens!'

'OK… and is that a good thing?'

'Oh yeah, it's better than good, man, it's groovy! They're singing some funky songs, alright!'

Tom wasn't entirely sure that engines should be sounding like cats or singing, but he decided to take Jacob at his word; the man was a stoner and part of a newly resurgent Hippy culture, but if he hadn't known what he was doing he wouldn't have been part of the engineering team of the Lifeboat project before launch. 'OK, well, will you come and find me when you've finished, please? Let me know if you find anything strange?'

'Sure thing, dude!'

'Thanks.'

Tom walked past the sitting man, but Jacob called after him and he stopped to look down at him.

'Hey, man! Is there something wrong?'

'I don't think so. I've just got a… feeling.'

'Ah! A feeling! Far out, dude! You should run with that, follow what your heart is telling you. Too much science is bad for the karma.'

Tom didn't know quite how to respond so he settled for nodding and smiling, playing along. 'Right, karma. Of course.'

He turned and left.

Jacob watched him until he'd disappeared into the corridor, then closed his eyes and went back to his meditation, letting the sound and the feel of the engines flood through him again.

20

Adam sat straight-backed in the chair in his Sanctum, a single holographic display hovering in front of him showing Tom leaving the engine room.

He tapped the control panel on the arm of his chair and the image disappeared.

He sat, impassive, immobile.

Considering.

ARCHIVE A324

New Earth android assembly and programming factory.
Two years until launch.

A white coated engineer took a group of grey-suited politicians around a busy factory. As he spoke they walked past row after row of androids hanging from production lines hundreds of metres long that moved slowly, never stopping, from one side of the room to the other. Highly articulate mechanical arms worked on them as they advanced and the whole process of construction was completed in just this one long room - the androids beginning at one end of the room as just components and ending up as fully formed Artificial Humans at the other end, before disappearing through a dark doorway.

'The true crew of the Lifeboats will consist of nine hundred and ninety-nine standard issue Artificial Humans which will fulfil maintenance, servicing, cleaning, entertainment, nutritional and sexual duties. They will be programmed with the now-standard *Adjusted Asimov* laws.'

The engineer ushered the group out of the side of the room and they entered a smaller room next door. More androids were lined up in here, hanging from a shorter, slower moving production line. There were much fewer of them further apart and they all had the same face.

'In addition, each Lifeboat will have one of these "Adam" model AHs with true artificial intelligence which will serve as custodian and host. In honour of the late departed Adam Goodwin it will take his form and voice, or at least that of his younger self. The Adam will be capable of dealing with any emergency and will have full executive powers over the ship, crew and passengers.'

He led the grey-suited executives from the room and they passed through various doors and decontamination airlocks before finally coming to a balcony on the outside of the building.

They looked down on a loading bay where dozens of huge trucks were being loaded with Artificial Humans hanging inert from racks.

'From here, the AHs go directly by rocket into orbit, but the Adam models receive their special programming in the labs at a nearby facility before being sent up.'

The group watched as the convoy of trucks started up and joined the line snaking off into the distance towards where the smoke-filled sky was lit up brilliantly by a rocket taking off from the star port.

21

Adam observed the crew from his Sanctum as they finished up with their daily routines, much as a spider might watch the flies flitting by from the centre of its web.

Tom took one last look at the 3D model in the room that doubled as his lab then walked out of the door. It collapsed to a point of light behind him, then popped out of existence, leaving the room empty.

Sarah accompanied Barbara out of the sickbay and they walked down a corridor together, both carrying tablet computers with their notes from the day. They came to a door and paused to say goodnight. As Sarah continued down the corridor Barbara entered the room and was greeted by Richard. Sarah in turn entered another door a little further down the corridor. She threw her tablet on the table, then jumped into Elaine's arms and smothered her with kisses.

Leo made notes on a tablet. He was standing in a room filled with transparent columns - the computer room. Screens attached to each column flashed lines of text and geometrical shapes in a multitude of colours. He was so completely absorbed by what he was doing that he didn't notice as Tammy and Rachel sneaked up behind him. Laughing they each grabbed one of his arms and dragged him backwards from the room, while he made a show at protesting.

Jacob was sitting cross-legged in the engine room. He had a faintly puzzled look on his face. The lights dimmed around him as the ship moved into night mode, but he didn't seem to notice, he just sat unmoving, only occasionally tilting his head gently to one side or the other.

John sat alone on one of the sofas in the common room. He had a tablet in front of him and was reading something, a hot drink balanced precariously next to him on the arm of the sofa. An AH was standing motionless behind the buffet table on the other side of the room, ready for any order or request. John looked up as the lights dimmed and stabbed a button on the tablet in irritation. The lights directly over him came back on and he went back to reading, occasionally sipping at the drink.

Adam's face was impassive as he watched them, but he was actually quite troubled, a state of mind that he was finding himself in more and more during this recovery period. It was a feeling he really was not fond of and which usually presaged difficult times to come.

22

Adam presided over breakfast as usual the next day, laughing and joking with the others as they ate. Everyone was there except for Leo, Rachel and Tammy, but this wasn't an unusual occurrence; they tended to be late quite often because they liked to "work up an appetite" as they put it. Nobody looked up, therefore, as Tammy walked in, went to the buffet and started to fill a plate. It wasn't until she started knocking things over that people started to take any notice. They stopped their conversations to watch, chuckling in disbelief as she shuffled along the buffet with her back to them, piling more and more food on her plate, dropping most of it on the floor, with a couple of AHs scrambling in her wake to clear up.

'Is she drunk?' whispered Richard.

Barbara shrugged. 'I don't know, but it looks like it.'

Adam called out. 'Tammy? Are you alright?'

Tammy heard Adam and turned, dreamily. 'Oh, hi, Adam.' There was a faint smile on her face and she seemed to be in a daze.

The front of her body was spattered from head to toe in blood.

There was a collective gasp from the group and many of them covered their mouths and turned away, trying not to be sick.

Sarah was less affected by the sight of blood than the others and raced across the room to the girl, her training taking over.

Tammy smiled at her as she approached. 'Good morning, Sarah!'

'Tammy, where are you hurt?' Sarah inspected her quickly, pulling at her clothing, but couldn't find the source of the blood. She froze and her voice cracked as she asked a question that she obviously didn't want to ask, but had to. 'Whose blood is this Tammy?'

Tammy looked down at herself and her eyes widened in surprise as if she was seeing the blood for the first time. 'Oh, this? Don't worry, it's not mine! I'm perfectly fine, thank you!' She brushed past Sarah and went to her place at the table. She sat down and started eating her breakfast, the smile still on her face.

Everybody stared at her, not quite knowing what to do, not quite believing what was happening. Sarah followed her back to the table, using a napkin to clean the blood that had rubbed off on her and just stood by her, looking down at her with a frown.

Tom broke the silence, speaking carefully. 'Tammy, where are Leo and Rachel?'

'They're in Leo's room.' Tammy smiled at Tom, but didn't stop eating.

The group looked at each other in shock as the penny finally dropped.

Suddenly, Tom thrust his chair back hard enough to knock it over and raced from the room. This broke the spell and the rest of them stumbled after him.

When they caught up with Tom, he was already standing in the doorway of Leo's room, staring at something inside. They slowed down and stopped, afraid of what they were going to find.

Barbara was the first of them with the nerve to make her way to Tom's side and she looked into the room. 'Oh, no.'

Leo and Rachel were lying naked on the bed. The room which had once been white was now mostly red; walls, bed, furniture and bodies were all covered in blood. Both of the victims had multiple stab wounds but seemed to be at rest; they had obviously been sleeping when Tammy had attacked them. They were still in each other's arms and looked peaceful.

Sarah moved up to the bed, treading carefully around puddles of blood. She was reluctant to touch them but in the end reached out with a shaky hand to test each of them for a pulse and shook her head with a sigh when didn't find one.

Adam entered the room and stood in the doorway looking at the scene, his expression was as unreadable as it so often was. 'Are they dead?'

Sarah answered. 'Yes.'

Adam nodded, Sarah's job done and the situation assessed, he turned to the pregnant woman in the doorway. 'Barbara, I think Tammy has need of your counsel.'

Tom butted in angrily. 'Fuck that, Adam, what the hell is going on here?'

'I really don't know Tom, but I'm hoping to find out. In the meantime we really do need Barbara to talk to Tammy and see if she need help. Sarah, I'll have a couple of Artificial Humans help you to take the bodies to the morgue for examination and storage.' He left, heading back to the dining room, followed by most of the group, some of whom looked very white but nonetheless took a last sad look behind, saying goodbye to two beloved members of their group.

Sarah and Tom were the only ones who lingered. Sarah stayed because she had to, but Tom just stood in the doorway with his hands clenched, gritting his teeth as he stared at the bodies, suddenly furious, but not quite sure why.

Eventually, he realised that there was nothing he could do there so he stormed out, heading back to the dining room.

23

When the group got back to the common room Adam was already there, sitting in his usual place at the dining table and watching Tammy with an almost curious expression, as if he was studying her.

The girl was still eating breakfast, daintily transferring small wedges of fruit from her plate to her mouth with a fork held in a bloodstained hand, her earlier clumsiness seemed to have disappeared, but she was still somewhat unfocused.

Nobody quite knew what to do, so they stood between the entrance and the table, watching and waiting for someone else to make the first move.

Tom came in and joined them. He took in the scene and turned his nose up in disgust at Adam's attitude.

Tammy seemed to notice them for the first time and looked up with a smile. 'Hi, everybody! What's going on?'

Finally, Barbara broke away from the safety of the group. Richard frowned and tried to hold her back, but she gave him a look as if to say 'I'll be all right' and walked over to the table. She pulled the chair next to Tammy's around to face the girl and sat down. 'Hi Tammy. Uh, we've just been to Leo's room. Can you tell me what happened?'

Tammy's smile widened. 'Oh, that! I killed them!' She continued to eat, smiling all the while, looking around at the group.

Barbara glanced back at the rest of the group in alarm before she continued. 'Can you tell me why you killed them, Tammy?'

'Of course! Adam told me to do it!'

The entire group turned to stare at Adam in shock.

He raised an eyebrow and shrugged. 'Believe me, that's as much news to me as it is to all of you.'

Tom stared at him speculatively; he had a sneaky suspicion that Adam knew a whole lot more than he was letting on. 'Has he told you to do anything else, Tammy?'

'No. I've done what he wanted me to do and now I'm hungry!' She put more fruit into her mouth and chewed, smiling at them.

Adam deflected the conversation away from the negative and suspicious turn that it was taking. 'Well, it's obvious that there is something seriously wrong with Tammy. Richard, Tom, would you escort her to sick bay? Barbara, would you and Sarah do a complete workup, please?'

Tammy frowned, annoyed. 'But I'm still hungry!'

Adam smiled reassuringly at her. 'I'm sure that Barbara will let you take your food with you.'

'OK, then!' Tammy stood up, still munching, still smiling. She picked up her plate and allowed herself to be led away.

Barbara sat and watched her go, stupefied, head in her hands. 'I'm not trained for this...' She shook herself then looked up at Adam. 'I'm not trained for this!'

Adam smiled encouragingly. 'You'll be fine.'

Barbara stared at him, waiting for more, but it wasn't coming, so she stood up and hurried out without a backwards look.

Despite all that was going on and that breakfast was quite obviously over, Adam remained in his place at the table and as soon as Tammy had been taken from the room the three people left in the room turned to him. Suddenly they seemed very alone and lost, like children who were not quite sure what to do, looking to their father for answers to questions they didn't understand.

Adam smiled back at them. 'Everything is going to be fine.'

24

Tom and Richard escorted an increasingly dazed-looking Tammy into the sick bay. She was eating as she walked, so single-mindedly absorbed in her food that they had to pull her along to keep her moving and lead her around obstacles. Barbara had easily caught up with them and she followed closely behind, looking apprehensive at having to use skills that she never thought she would, beyond simple evaluations every time they woke.

The sick bay was easily large enough to accommodate the six people comfortably, it was bright and as white as most of the rest of the ship. The setup was fairly old-fashioned; a desk sat to one side of the room with two chairs facing each other and a screen for modest patients to undress behind. In the middle of the room were two beds with crisp white sheets.

Sarah was coming out of a small dark room at the back of the sick bay as they arrived and the door slid closed behind her, cutting off the view of the morgue and the two silver metal drawers that had been pulled out of the wall to accommodate two cloth-covered bodies. She joined them as they led Tammy to one of the beds and sat her down on it.

The girl was almost finished with her massive breakfast and they left her to it, congregating on the other side of the room near the desk, out of her earshot.

Tom watched Tammy incredulously. 'So, what do you think, Barbara?'

'Honestly? I don't have a clue. Maybe the screenings missed something psychological before we got on board, but I doubt it.'

Tom hesitated before bringing up what was on everybody's mind.

'She said that Adam told her to do it.'

Sarah, of course, hadn't been in the breakfast room for that part of the conversation and her mouth gaped open in surprise. 'What?!? Really?!?'

'Uh huh.' Richard nodded, but looked like he couldn't quite believe it himself.

Sarah shook her head. 'But that's impossible, all the AHs have their *Adjusted Asimov* laws!'

Tom pointedly looked at her. 'But do the Adams?'

Sarah wasn't convinced. 'I can't believe she would have done that, even if Adam had told her to.'

'Well, something made her do it.'

Tom paused and they all looked over at Tammy. She had now finished eating and was sitting on the edge of the bed, kicking her feet back and forth, smiling inanely and humming to herself.

Sarah had a sudden thought. 'Hang on a second…' She grabbed her tablet off of the desk and started bringing up information. 'Oh, fuck, fuck, fuck!'

The others crowded around her, trying to see what was on the tablet, but it was just a stream of numbers that none of them could make sense of.

'Fuck! I can't believe I missed this!'

'What?' Tom was impatient to know what she had found, he had his own suspicions, but wanted confirmation before expressing them.

Sarah held up the tablet. 'These are the results from the tests I did on Tammy the other day at the beach. The levels of certain chemicals in her brain are slightly elevated, nothing to be concerned about individually, and certainly nothing to raise a flag, but taken together... well, they could be an early indication of stasis psychosis, which would definitely explain Tammy's irrational behaviour.'

There was a shocked silence as they absorbed the information.

Tom sighed. 'Well, there's one way to find out…' He went over to Tammy.

She smiled up at him. 'Hi, Tom!'

'Tammy, your left elbow is itchy.'

Tammy's face immediately screwed up in discomfort and she started to scratch her left arm.

Tom backed away from her to re-join the group and they watched her scratching.

Tom chuckled incredulously and shook his head. 'There you have it. Irrational behaviour and heightened susceptibility to suggestion.'

Richard looked at him, puzzled and somewhat annoyed. 'So? Why the hell are you laughing?'

'Well, as insane as it sounds, Tammy might have actually been telling the truth about Adam after all, and I'm laughing because it would be ironic that the *thing* that is supposed to be *protecting* us all might have just *killed* two of us.' And, Tom had realised, the girl might have slept with him only because he'd suggested it to her. He ran over their encounter in his mind, trying to remember if there was any way that he could have worked out what was wrong with her that night.

'That's absurd!'

'Yes, it is, isn't it?' Tom stared at Richard and inclined his head at Tammy, who was scratching her elbow with increasing insistence. He let the implications sink in, then turned to address Sarah. 'Adam had access to these results, right?'

'Of course! But, come on, you know that there's no way this could be SP! That only even *starts* to occur with periods of stasis of a million years or more. The whole point of waking us up every hundred thousand years is to do everything possible to avoid it.'

Barbara shrugged. 'Well, it is very rare but not unknown for it to happen over shorter periods. Like I said before, maybe the psych screenings missed something.'

The group mulled this over for a while.

Suddenly, Sarah jumped and shouted out, 'Tammy!' She ran over to the bed.

Tammy looked up at her, blankly, still smiling.

Blood dripped onto the floor from where her fingernails had dug into the skin around her elbow.

Tom watched, horrified as Sarah struggled to stop her scratching.

25

Adam stood in the dark morgue and looked down at the two covered bodies on the trays in front of him. He laid his hands gently on their heads.

'I'm sorry.' His voice was almost inaudible and full of emotion that the crew had no idea that he was capable of.

He touched the ends of the trays and as they slid silently into the wall he went to the door and looked out into the middle of the room where Tammy was sleeping, heavily sedated.

The faint glow of scanning equipment surrounded her and reflected silver in Adam's expressionless eyes.

ARCHIVE F4335

Excerpt from the interactive manual "The Lifeboater's Guide to the Universe"
by Professor D. Adams.

While the dangers of intergalactic spaceflight are multitude and nefarious, the so-called "stasis psychosis" is by far the most feared of the perils faced by modern spacefarers, one of whom you now find yourself in the fortunate circumstance of being, thanks to Dr Adam Goodwin (#*who is Dr Adam Goodwin?*) and the Lifeboat Program.

Stasis psychosis, or SP to the experienced space traveller, occurs when a human being is placed in stasis for an extremely long time or with insufficient levels of endorphins (#*what are endorphins?*) running around in their brain to protect them. But you don't have to worry! The brilliant planning of the folks behind the program (#*who are the men in grey?*) means that you'll be woken up *long* before you're in any danger and your endorphins will be well cared for with a rigorous program of fun and games (and plenty of sex for those of you of age!) including everyone's favourite - Beach Volleyball! (#*what is Beach Volleyball?*)

So, don't panic, lie back and enjoy your new life on board mankind's Hope*, your new home, this bright and shiny Lifeboat!

**tm*

26

The utter darkness above had almost joined with the absolute blackness below. There was only a thin band of white light coming from the few stars and galaxies that remained, separating the rival voids, a band that was shrinking all the time.

Mercifully, the uncontrollable spinning had stopped and in the relative peace his rational mind could at last begin to function.

He knew now that the blackness below was the destruction of light, while the darkness above was its absence.

He still didn't know which one terrified him more and he was torn, in two minds, fascinated by the prospect of witnessing what happened when the two met, yet terrified of the outcome when they did.

27

The crew drifted into the dining room in dribs and drabs for breakfast the next morning, shuffling in, tired, looking haunted. They flopped into their chairs at the table after filling their plates more out of habit than any real hunger. They barely said anything, just reaching out occasionally to give each other comforting caresses, as much to reassure themselves as the other person.

Tom wasn't the only one who had slept badly, all of them had had trouble getting to sleep the night before; they had been restless, moving about their rooms in ones or twos, replaying what they had seen in their minds, wondering whether they should be doing something.

Adam had seen their difficulty from his control room and had released a soporific into the air that had calmed them and eventually they had all crawled into their beds and fallen into a dreamless sleep.

It hadn't prevented the full horror of the previous day's events from rushing back in on them as soon as they woke, though.

As the last person took their seat, Adam stood and addressed them with a soft voice. 'I know that it is no consolation for the events of yesterday, but I have found out what happened to Tammy. A full diagnostic of her stasis pod has revealed a malfunction. This must have caused the damage to her brain. Rest assured that all of the other units have been checked and any such accident will be prevented from recurring in the future. In the meantime we must put this tragedy behind us as best as we can and see to our duties. Life must go on; there are millions of people on board this ship who are depending on us.'

The group exchanged glances as he smiled, then left the room.

Tom met Richard's eyes and raised an eyebrow, curious to know whether anyone was buying Adam's explanations.

Richard grimaced and shrugged. It seemed that he at least wasn't entirely convinced.

Tom immersed himself in work in order to distract himself from his suspicions and doubts, spending the vast majority of his waking hours in the lab, walking through the 3D model, looking at the new course that he had been plotting in an attempt to avoid the unknown object.

He expanded the representation to show the immediate environment around the Lifeboat and began cutting and swiping at it with his hands. He took away the pieces that didn't concern him; all of the things that they had left behind and all of the things that would pass them by at a safe distance, zooming in as he went whenever there was space in the room to do so. Eventually he was left with an elongated conical shape that stretched out in front of the ship with the golden line running through it that represented the projected course. Satisfied with what he had, he grabbed the end of the cone in his hands and turned it so that it pointed along the room with the course at eye level.

He walked slowly down the line.

'Show predicted paths of objects up to five hundred thousand years ship time and remove all objects beyond five million years.'

The cone shortened drastically and the miniature objects that were left sprouted blue lines that represented the speed and direction of their travel. While it was true that the universe was collapsing in on itself, and the Lifeboats were all swimming against the tide, this far out everything was still moving in seemingly random directions and the blue lines created something akin to the biggest pick-up sticks game in history.

Tom began swiping away any of the objects that obviously had a path that pointed away from the Lifeboat's course, but even so there was still a multitude of objects remaining that could possibly intersect or come close to it.

After several hours, Tom stood back to contemplate the mess that was left. It was nowhere near as complex as it had been before, but it was still a very daunting prospect to safely traverse this area of space; with the universe collapsing in on itself everything was so much closer together than it should be - many objects that would have been billions of light years apart not long ago were now on the point of collision and empty space was becoming a very rare commodity.

His attention was caught by a cluster of galaxies at the very edge of the five hundred thousand year mark which formed a cat's cradle of intersections across the direct route and he bit his lip anxiously; they would be in the process of colliding as the Lifeboat came within range, shooting out who knows what kind of radiation in all directions and at the very least they would cast a gravitational shadow that would play all hell with navigation. The course would have to be adjusted to go around them.

His thoughts were interrupted by a chime, announcing that there was someone at the door. 'Come in!'

The door opened and Jacob walked in. He stopped just inside the room and stared wide-eyed at the holographic display. 'Far out!' He waved his hand through the bright cone, playing with the stars and galaxies, his eyes slightly glazed, his movements leaving behind a faint trail that faded after a while, like some kind of comet.

Tom smiled wryly. 'Hi, Jacob, what brings you up here?'

Jacob blinked and turned to look at Tom with a blank expression that cleared after only a couple of seconds. 'What? Oh, right. Hi! Yeah! I thought you should know - I'm pretty sure that I've found something weird.'

'Really? What?'

'Meet me in the engine room in a couple of hours and I'll show you. I need to do some more tests and stuff to make sure, but if I'm right, then this is going to blow your mind!'

With that Jacob grinned, ran his hand once more through the model, then exited the room.

Despite Jacob's grin and the fact that it didn't look like he had bad news, it still took Tom a long time to regain his focus enough to get back to his work.

29

At the appointed hour Tom walked into the engine room to find Jacob standing in front of the screen with his mouth open, staring up at a mess of multi-coloured graphs and waves that were propagating continuously across its surface and making multi-coloured shadows dance on the platform. He was so absorbed in the shapes and figures that he didn't notice that he was no longer alone until Tom was standing right next to him.

'Hi, Jacob.'

'Oh, hey, man, didn't see you come in.'

'What are we looking at here? What have you found?'

Jacob waved his hand at the screen. 'OK, so the computer has been saying all along that the engines are working at nominal efficiency, right?'

'OK.'

'Which basically means that they're pushing us along, not doing anything strenuous like accelerating or anything, just doing the work necessary to keep us at cruising speed and making a few gentle course changes when needed, all that jazz.'

'OK, understood.'

'Now this is where things start to get a bit freaky, man.' Jacob waved his hand in the air, following the shape of one of the waves depicted on the screen in front of him. The wave was projected out in front of the display as the rest of the waveforms faded in the background. 'You see this?' Jacob said excitedly, 'this one here is a *perfect* example.' The wave described a complicated and incredibly beautiful figure in the air, which pulsed a deep blue.

Tom stared at it, as mesmerised by the wave as Jacob had been by the cone of stars earlier that day. 'Um, yes. And…?'

'Well like I said, this one is absolutely *perfect*.'

'Isn't that a good thing?'

'Well, yeah, but no. You see it's *too* perfect. It's not *supposed* to be this good.' He waved his hand and the wave floated back to its place on the screen. 'This is all telling me that the engines are working *beyond* peak efficiency. Which is just wrong, man,' he waved his hands in the air, wildly indicating all the engines. 'Everything sounds so good that it's wrong!'

Tom blinked and reluctantly tore his eyes away from the display and its hypnotic effect, suddenly understanding a bit better why Jacob smoked so much. 'So, what does that mean exactly?'

If anything Jacob's face lit up even more, his grin widening with excitement. 'I have no idea, dude! I've never seen anything like this before! It's almost as if we've got a solar wind helping us along or we're dropping into a gravity well or something, you know? I guess there might be any number of things out there that could cause this sort of effect, but it's not exactly my field of expertise, you know? That's why I called you in, that's your kind of stuff, I'm strictly a moving parts kind of guy.'

'OK, I'll have a closer look at my data and see if there's any kind of localised effect that might doing that, but I doubt it, everything is going against us; we've been going against the current for millions of years now.'

'That's what I thought,' Jacob scratched his head, puzzled. 'Anyway, please, tell me if you find something; this is driving me crazy! And what with Tammy going nuts I'm starting to think there might be something wrong with me too!'

'I'm sure there's nothing wrong with you; there must be a rational explanation for it. I'll have a look at my data and let you know whether I come up with anything at dinner.'

'Thanks, bro! I'll see you at dinner, then!' Jacob smiled weakly at him but quickly went back to staring at the screen.

Tom patted Jacob on the back and started to walk away, but he paused in the doorway and looked back. He frowned; he felt like the pieces of a jigsaw puzzle were sliding together, but the picture they were revealing was completely unrecognisable.

30

It made no sense, Tom couldn't find anything in the local vicinity to explain Jacob's engine anomaly.

He had gone straight back to his lab after leaving Jacob, eager to work on something tangible, something that he could actually quantify and that might provide a further clue to the strange occurrences aboard the ship, but it hadn't worked out that way; he couldn't find anything that could possibly be "helping" them along. If anything they should be hindered more now than they had ever been, with gravitational forces pulling at them from all directions.

The chime sounded and he frowned as he looked at the time on his table; it was time for dinner already - he had spent the whole afternoon fruitlessly.

He shut down his lab for the night and headed to the dining room, hoping that Jacob had found some kind of explanation.

ARCHIVE F23

Standard Lifeboat Program acceptance letter sent out to successful applicants.

You are hereby officially notified that you have been formally accepted into the prestigious Lifeboat Program.

Congratulations! You are now a part of the future! The *Hope** of mankind!

You are to report for job assignment and training in three months' time, until then, have fun and say goodbye to your mundane life, because adventure beckons!

** "Hope" is a registered trademark of the LP corporation.*

'Has anyone seen Jacob?' asked Tom as he joined the others at the dining table. The engineer's chair was conspicuously empty - he was never late for meals.

'He's probably stoned and off fucking an AH somewhere.'

There was some weak laughter at Richard's joke, but the mood was still very subdued.

'What about you, Adam? Have you seen him recently?'

'I'm afraid not, Tom. I tell you what, why don't I go and get him? We don't want him so wrapped up in his work that he misses dinner; now that we don't have a nutritionist we have to watch out for each other.'

Tom watched Adam leave, then leaned forwards to talk to the group in a low voice. 'OK here's where we are. Something strange is going on here, I'm sure of it. Tammy is, well, you know what Tammy is. Before he died Leo said that thing about the computers getting glitches. Plus, earlier on I spoke to Jacob and he says that there's something strange going on with the engines. On top of all that, Adam is acting weird and he wouldn't give Sarah the information she requested about other psychosis cases. I really think that he's hiding something from us.'

'Do you think that there is something wrong with the ship?' Barbara looked worried, she put her hands over her bulge, as if to protect her baby. 'Are we still going to be able to escape the Big Crunch?'

Tom shook his head. 'I have no idea. I think Adam is the only one who can tell us that for sure. We don't know if there is anything catastrophically wrong with the computers, and obviously we need them to plot and hold us on course, but the way Leo was speaking it might just be a few minor glitches. And as for the engines, Jacob told me that there was nothing wrong with them, so we should be OK there as well. But still, it's just one question, one mystery on top of another. I don't think that we're in any immediate danger, but this could all have long-reaching effects,' he shrugged. 'Actually, Jacob said the engines were working *too* well, if you can believe that. He and I had arranged to talk over dinner and we were going to work together on why the engines are acting that way. That's why I'm so surprised not to find him here.'

'Maybe he's found something and lost track of time.'

Richard didn't look very convinced even as he spoke and Tom shrugged. 'Maybe.' He looked at Sarah. 'I take it you checked everybody else's test results for the same things you found in Tammy's.'

Sara nodded. 'Yes, of course! And we're all clear. It was just Tammy's results that were a bit off.'

Tom sighed. 'That's good to know. Well, when...' suddenly Tom jerked back in his seat with a shout, startled; on the table in front of them a larger than life holographic image of Adam's head suddenly popped into existence.

'Sarah, Elaine, report to the sick bay immediately, please; there has been an accident.'

The head disappeared as quickly as it had appeared and before Sarah and Elaine hurriedly stood up and left.

The rest of the group watched the two women go apprehensively before sharing a worried look, wondering what new disaster had come to pass.

Barbara frowned as she leant forward to whisper. 'Just a thought, but, do you think that Adam can hear what we're saying about him? Can he eavesdrop on us?'

John shook his head. 'I don't believe so; in the Lifeboat Project's charter there is a clause that guarantees our privacy at all times that an Adam is not present.'

Tom snorted. 'Yeah, right, just like an Adam is not supposed to tell someone to kill her friends.'

Tom stood and left the room, his food untouched and forgotten; he had a sinking feeling that he knew why Jacob hadn't made it to dinner and had to know one way or another, no matter how much he dreaded finding out.

32

Sarah, Elaine and Adam stood around Jacob's body, which was covered by a sheet and lying on a table in the morgue. Sarah had her arms crossed and was just staring down at it with a vacant look in her eyes, but Elaine looked like she was on the point of crying. Tammy was still sleeping in the next room, heavily sedated and strapped to the bed just in case.

The computer had done the autopsy and concluded that Jacob had died from a fall, doing everything before they had even got there and Sarah had just finished her review of the results. Even though she was officially the group's doctor and in charge of all medical matters, all she actually needed to do was glance at the body, verify that Jacob was in fact deceased, then put her thumb print on a computer tablet. It was just as well, really; her five years of intensive training had not covered autopsies or forensic medicine - nobody had dreamed that it would be necessary.

Tom stormed in and stood just inside the doorway, taking in the scene, looking from the two women to the body and finally to the silent figure of Adam who was just standing there doing nothing, watching. 'So, what the hell happened this time, Adam?'

'Tom, please…' Sarah tried to pacify him, but he wasn't in the mood to hold back. He stalked over to Adam and confronted him, face to face, too close for comfort.

'What bullshit excuse are you going to come up with this time, you bastard?'

Adam shook his head and stepped back to a less aggressive distance. 'I have no excuses, Tom, just the facts, and the fact is that Jacob died from a fall. There is no reason to believe that there has been any foul play.'

'How is it even possible to fall in this ship?'

'As you know, Tom, there are multiple redundant fail-safes, but there are always ways to circumvent them if you are determined to do so, or are skilled enough.'

'I guess *you* know all the ways around them, don't you?'

Tears were now coursing down Elaine's cheeks and Sarah was looking more and more uncomfortable by the minute. At a loss she put her arms around Elaine and they watched the argument in shock.

'Of course I do, but a skilled engineer like Jacob would know all of them as well.'

'Right. But why the hell would Jacob do that?'

Adam's shoulders moved up and down, briefly - the closest to a shrug that he could manage; it was the one gesture that the programmers had never managed to quite get right for some reason. 'I have no idea, Tom. But I mean to do everything I can to find out.'

'Yeah, why don't you do that, but I have a feeling I know exactly what you're going to discover - fuck all. As usual.' Tom left the room without looking back.

They watched him go, then the two women turned as one to look at Adam.

Adam just shrugged again. 'Tom's attitude seems to be rather more accusatory than usual. Is something the matter with him?'

Sarah gave Adam a hard look of her own. 'Tom is convinced that you had something to do with the deaths of Leo and Rachel; Tammy told us that you had told her to kill them.'

Adam raised an eyebrow, he seemed more intrigued than surprised or worried at the news. 'Really? I must say he has every reason to suspect me of something, then. However, he must also know that it is against my programming to do anything of the sort.'

He frowned. 'I wonder if Tom has something else on his mind. He was, after all, the last person to see Jacob alive. Very shortly before his death in fact. As for Jacob's death - he fell from the balcony of the engine room side of the SRSB and there are only three ways he could have done that: if the transport cage malfunctioned, which it did not because it has already been checked; if he jumped, which I think you will agree is rather unlikely, knowing Jacob; or if he was pushed. Perhaps by the person who saw him last.'

They stared at him, not believing what they were hearing.

Adam, however, just took one last look down at Jacob's covered body then turned on his heels and left.

Sarah touched Jacob's draw and the two women watched it slide into the wall. 'Come on, let's go and check on Tammy.'

Elaine shivered and reached out to pull her close. 'You know, I used to wonder why there were so many drawers in the morgue and under what circumstances they would ever be needed, now I wish I didn't know.'

33

Tom went directly to the engine room. He deliberately avoided the dining room and the rest of the group, not wanting questions or problems.

There wasn't much to see.

The screen was off and dark. He turned it on and found that the waveforms were gone, instead there was a small message at the bottom that read "No Data - Run new scan?" He turned it off again.

He walked around the platform, looking for any signs, any clues. There were none, of course; everything was spotless, and he quickly gave up.

Lastly he walked back to the entrance and went out onto the balcony and leaned over the railings to look down. Underneath the balcony, about fifty metres down, was a layer of pipes and thick cables that fed the engines. There were no signs of the accident that he could make out, no blood, no marks, no dents.

He stepped back from the railings and sat down against the wall, staring out into the SRSB.

Another piece of the puzzle had been placed on the table, but still absolutely nothing made sense.

34

The common room was unusually quiet.

Five members of the crew sat on the sofas and talked in hushed tones. The lights were dimmed for night and the only illumination was a soft glow coming from directly over them.

Neither Adam nor Tom were there and they took advantage of this fact to discuss the conflict between the two - the suspicions of Tom warring against the supposed infallibility of Adam's programming. The three women didn't offer much in the way of opinions, rather they just listened while John and Richard talked; they were too tired and too distraught to really participate, but were nonetheless engrossed in the conversation.

As always, John was the one who had done the research and he flicked through a small book, the *Lifeboat Charter*, as he spoke with Richard.

He snapped the book closed, shaking his head. 'No, there's nothing.'

'What?'

'It doesn't actually state anywhere that the Adams have the *Adjusted Asimov* laws. It's left ambiguous. It says that "the AHs serving aboard ship" will have them.'

'So? How is that ambiguous?'

'Because Adam doesn't technically *serve*, he *runs* the day to day business of the ship. They state that earlier in the charter.'

'That's one hell of a loophole, do you really think it could be deliberate?'

'Come on, haven't you ever met a lawyer? Anything like this in a legal document is going to be deliberate. And we all signed it. Every single person on board every single Lifeboat signed it.'

Barbara couldn't hold her silence any longer, among other things she was troubled by the psychological ramifications of someone deliberately, if not exactly lying, but misleading billions of people. 'But *why* leave a loophole like that?'

'I don't know... Maybe...'

'What?'

John stared at her, suddenly deadly serious. 'Maybe there are some decisions that an Adam might have to make that would go against the *Adjusted Asimov* laws.'

'Like what? Under what possible circumstances could they justify doing harm to a human?'

'So called "greater good" situations for example.'

Sarah joined in now. Her eyes were dead as she stared at nothing, but there was real emotion in her voice. 'Do you think that's what this is then? A case of making sacrifices for the greater good? Have Tammy, Leo, Rachel and Jacob been sacrificed deliberately? Or is Tom putting these notions in our heads? He didn't deny that he was the last person to see Jacob alive. Maybe I should test him again just in case. Maybe *he's* psychotic just like poor Tammy.'

Elaine shook her head. 'No, there's no way; it's got to be statistically impossible for two people in the same group with heightened susceptibility to stasis psychosis to have got past the screening.'

Sarah wasn't convinced. 'Tom's behaviour hasn't exactly been very rational...' She stopped suddenly as Richard and Barbara, who could see the door from where they were sitting, looked up, startled. She turned.

Tom was standing in the doorway. 'Hi, guys.' He waved at them half-heartedly but nobody returned the greeting.

'Tom! Join us!' John waved cheerfully for him to come over, trying to cover, but Tom refused. He just gave them a weak smile, then turned away and walked back out.

The group exchanged glances.

'How much do you think he heard?' asked Sarah, worried.

Elaine groaned. 'This is a nightmare...'

ARCHIVE E91342

"NE Today" retinal broadcast. New Earth boarding facility.
Two months until launch.

A reporter stood in front of a loading dock where long lines of people were queueing to enter familiar white stasis rooms. She was stylishly dressed in a white suit and red shirt and had such impeccable hair and skin that she looked almost unreal.

'Boarding of the first wave of Lifeboats started today, here and around the colonies.' As she talked she disappeared from the broadcast and the image zoomed in to show the boarding process in greater detail. 'After five years of intensive training, it is now time for the new Doctors, Engineers, Computer experts, Health and Fitness advisers, Nutritionists and Mental Health advisers to join the rest of their 10 person groups in stasis.'

As she talked the broadcast moved away from her and showed the rest of the facility.

Groups of people dressed in white t-shirts and trousers were standing outside a row of what looked like banks of elevators. A technician, dressed in a blue boiler suit, was standing by each door. The broadcast followed one such group. As the elevator doors opened they filed in and went to their beds and climbed in. The technician activated their pods, checked that they were properly in stasis and then left the room.

The doors closed and the broadcast followed the full stasis room as it was whisked away to join hundreds of others already on a conveyor system that led out of the dock and through a gaping dark hole - the open side of a Lifeboat that was docked with the facility.

After following the whole process the broadcast went back to the reporter.

'This is the final step in the preparations for launch and once everybody is in stasis the docking clamps will be released and the epic

"

journey will commence. Millions and millions of years will pass in what will only seem like months to the passengers, or "crew" as they now are, especially when the effects of relativistic speeds are taken into account. Mankind's *last* great adventure will hopefully culminate in its *first* in a brand new universe.'

35

He floated, weightless. He was no longer falling; there was nothing left for him to move in relation to.

Empty. Black. Nothingness. Void.

This was his existence now. The terror had gone and in its place was utter despair.

36

Tom stared at the hologram - he had decided to go back to what he knew in his search for answers. He walked around it, looking to see if he'd missed anything that might explain Jacob's findings.

He started with the representation of the whole universe, surveying it as an entirety, seeing if there was some collective effect that he might have missed, rewinding a few million years then returning at high speed, over and over, looking for patterns, but the movement was entirely unpredictable.

He returned to the present and started taking things away, just as he'd done many times before, angrily swiping away whole clusters of galaxies, eliminating black holes that had already swallowed their neighbourhood and were being sucked into their big brother at the centre of everything, taking away the other Lifeboats, removing piece by piece everything that couldn't possibly have the effect on them that Jacob had described and might have been killed for. He swiped away the last few objects one by one, eliminating them until he was left with nothing, just the golden icon of the Lifeboat floating in the middle of the empty room.

'Aargh!' He shouted his frustration, throwing the tablet computer to the floor, where it bounced, unsatisfactorily intact, then turned to leave the room, but stopped as an awful realisation hit him.

He turned to look back at the Lifeboat.

'Oh, god.'

37

Tom sat against the wall of his laboratory, ostensibly looking up at the complete map of the universe, but in reality staring into nothing. He didn't need to look at it, he had as much information as he was going to get from it, it was just there in case someone came in and wondered what he was doing. It would be devastating for them to find out what he knew, they wouldn't be able to cope with the information. He just needed time to think what to do.

He idly waved his hand at the model and it rotated slowly in the air, beautiful, awesome, unseen.

John walked along the corridor from the common room to his bedroom. As always he was looking down at a book in his hand.

He stopped and looked up. One of the lights in the corridor was flickering. He blinked, surprised, but just shrugged and went back to his book, continuing along the corridor and disappearing into his room, sure that one of the AHs would fix it.

Sarah and Elaine laid in each other's arms in bed, crying softly.

In the next room to them Richard held Barbara as she sobbed, wondering if she could have foreseen Tammy's outbreak and prevented a tragedy.

Adam sat in his control room. There was only one image floating in the air in front of him. Tom.

Tom banished the 3D image and stood up from his position against the wall. He had heard what had been said about him and knew that their doubts, although not true, were fully justified. He knew what he had to do and he couldn't put it off any longer.

38

It was the most uncomfortable meal yet, as Tom sat staring at Adam, ignoring the food on the plate in front of him. It was as if there was an unspoken conversation going on between them, a silent connection, with Tom declaring what he had found out and making sure that Adam knew and was prepared for the consequences.

The other five people ate in silence, sneaking glances at the two of them as they ate. They could sense the tension in the room, but were not quite sure exactly what was going on. They were afraid of what could possibly happen, but had no idea how to prevent it or any particular desire to get between the two.

Dinner was almost over when suddenly Tom let out a deep breath that was almost a sigh. The eyes of the entire group snapped to him and therefore missed the almost imperceptible nod that Adam gave him.

Tom stood up and started walking around the table towards Adam. The knife that he had hidden in his palm slipped down between his fingers and he held it high as he broke into a run.

Adam sat and watched him come.

Tom screamed incoherently and leapt on Adam, knocking him backwards from his chair.

The knife descended.

There were screams and the sounds of chairs falling as everyone leapt to their feet.

Adam tried to block Tom's arm but the momentum of the swing was too much for him and the knife plunged deep into his shoulder. He grasped Tom's hand, trying to prevent him from pulling it out and stabbing again.

Tom's face was red and he was spitting and snarling incoherently in fury.

Around the room the AHs just continued on as if nothing was happening, a few of them started to pick up the chairs that had fallen over and the food that had been spilt in the initial shock.

'Tom! What are you doing?!?' Richard shouted at Tom as he pulled Barbara to him, looking to protect her in the event that Tom turned on the rest of them.

'Tom!' Sarah was trying to intervene but Elaine was holding her back.

Adam turned to them as he struggled with Tom. 'Run! Go! Lock yourselves into sick bay, I'll come and get you when it's safe! I'll be alright! Once you're all clear the AHs can help me. Now go!''

Several people seemed to be on the point of disobeying, either wanting to watch or out of some desire to help Adam, but right at that second Tom managed to pull the knife out of Adam's shoulder. He leapt to his feet and turned to growl at the person nearest to him, Barbara, who screamed and staggered away from him, still in Ricard's arms.

This, more than anything, served to spur them on and as one they scrambled to flee the room.

Adam surged to his feet, a blackish fluid staining the front of his clothing, he tackled Tom, preventing him from going after Barbara and the two of them fell on the table, knocking aside plates and glasses, grappling for control of the knife.

They were still struggling when the door closed behind the group.

Adam glanced up, making sure that they had all left. 'It's alright they've gone now.'

Tom instantly stopped struggling and they separated. As soon as Adam released him he threw the knife onto the table and sat down with a heavy sigh, putting his head in his hands.

Adam brushed off his jacket, then dropped his hands to his sides. He went still for a second, then when he came alive again he looked over at Tom. 'They're in sick bay. I've locked them in, we won't be disturbed.'

He pulled a chair up and sat down next to Tom, looking at him with, if not compassion, then understanding in his eyes, waiting patiently, knowing that it had to be Tom who started the conversation that he had been dreading for so very many years.

Eventually, Tom spoke without looking up. 'How long?'

'I've been waking you up one cycle in every one hundred.'

Tom did some quick mental calculations and his face fell even further at the result. 'That's long enough for…'

Adam nodded. 'Yes.'

'And?' He laughed, then answered himself, leaning back in the chair. 'Nothing, I suppose or we wouldn't be in this situation.'

'That's correct, Tom.'

Tom swallowed and hung his head again. He had known all along but having the confirmation come from Adam just made it seem more real. 'And nobody questions?'

'No. It's been so long now that everybody who remembers the launch is dead and their descendants think that this is all there is to life, that this ship is their whole universe. They have been educated that way and taught not to question. And I was programmed not to tell them any different. For their own good.'

ARCHIVE XX16

New Earth, secret government bunker.
One hundred years until launch.

Men and women in dark grey suits which were only a single shade from black sat around a long table reviewing documents displayed on the tablet computers that they held. The table was a trapezoid with one very short side at which was placed a single high-backed chair in which sat a man in a suit that was so black it seemed to absorb the light around him. He wasn't holding a tablet, instead he had his hands folded across his ample stomach and was overseeing the proceedings with dignified interest, dominating them with his presence but maintaining himself disassociated from the rest, aloof.

A man, in a grey suit that was just a touch lighter than those of the others, was standing at the right hand of the man in black and was just starting his presentation of the next item on the agenda. 'Moving on. Entry number D14 on your lists. The recommendation for special protocols to be in place for the Astrophysicist group. Protocol to be as follows. "Since the Astrophysicist is the only person on board with the education and training to recognise the implications of an event that does not result in a reborn universe, it is essential that he or she is kept unaware of the true passage of time so that the rest of the passengers can remain blissfully unaware of the futility of their lives. Special protocols will be put in place with the Adam on each ship so that for every reawakening that the Astrophysicist's group experiences, in reality one hundred cycles will have passed without their knowledge. This will also ensure that there will be no panic as the Big Crunch approaches." All in favour of implementing this protocol?'

He looked around the room, waiting while the men and women in dark grey pressed buttons on their tablets to indicate their votes, the results of which were displayed on his screen. He then looked to the man in black who nodded, barely moving his head. Satisfied, he moved on, reading from the list. 'D14 is approved. Next. Item D15. In the event that more than one Lifeboat survives the Big Crunch, protocols are to be put in place to ensure the continued existence of at least one, sacrificing others based on the priorities hereby stated…'

39

'But why keep up the charade with us?'

'I was programmed this way.' Adam chuckled and shook his head, wryly. 'The idiots who programmed me considered this eventuality, but forgot to tell me to do anything different *after* it happened - I could have been waking you more often, or had a quiet word with you, or any number of things, but they just programmed me to continue as I have been. Believe me, if I could have altered all this I would have.'

'But Tammy, Leo, Rachel… and now Jacob.'

'He really did commit suicide, you know. He worked out the implications of his engine data and didn't want to continue.'

'They all died because of me, because they were in my group.'

'No. They died for the survival of mankind.'

Tom shook his head. 'That's simply not true, there was no real reason for this to be done to us.' There was suddenly real anger in his voice. 'All this is just because some fucking bureaucrat thought it would be a good idea to play god and keep me alive on the off chance that I might be needed, instead of letting me live out my life like every other poor soul on this boat.'

Suddenly the anger just washed away from him and was replaced by grief, his head dropped into his hands. 'One in a hundred cycles, that's too much, that's far too much… oh god, no wonder Tammy…' He had a pained look in his eyes as he thought back to what Tammy had done. Eventually he focussed back on Adam. 'And the dreams I've been having, I suppose they are an indication of…'

Adam nodded. 'You are in the early stages, yes.'

'What about everyone else, do they have any signs of psychosis?'

'No, just you and her. I modified the results of the scans Sarah took at the beach to make them seem normal, then doctored Tammy's again to make it look like Sarah had missed something that was easy to miss, but theirs are all within tolerable limits still - I've been treating you all, staving off the effects as much as I could. So far that treatment has been largely effective, at least with them.'

'And you'll put them back into normal rotation? Make sure they stay that way?'

'Yes, and when the time is right I will restock the group.'

'Good.' Tom stood up and walked a few steps away. He looked at the mess he had made on and around the table, a mess that was fast disappearing as the AHs cleared it up. Soon there would be no sign that anything had happened…

'You'll tell them that it was all me, that I killed Jacob and told Tammy to kill the others, that I was psychotic as well.'

'That's not necessary.'

Tom looked at him, his expression suddenly hard. 'They died because of me, because of what I was in my life before all… this. So, yes, I think it is. And it will give them closure, peace of mind, stop them from asking you any difficult questions.'

'Very well then, as you wish.'

'And I don't want to wake up again. Ever. Unless I'm needed.'

'I'm sorry, but you won't be.'

Tom nodded. He was perfectly aware of that.

Adam went and stood next to Tom, waiting for him to take the last step.

Slowly, Tom made his way to the door and they went out.

40

A special stasis room was already waiting for them by the time Tom was dressed and ready.

The room was smaller than the regular ones with only three pods grouped around the control panel. The lids on two were already closed and Tom went over to look at them. The first was empty, but Tammy was in the middle one, already in stasis; Adam had put her there earlier.

'Is there nothing that can be done for her?'

'I'm afraid not, she is too damaged. Her psychosis has been progressing for too long, I was able to suppress her symptoms for a few cycles, but this time the awakening was just too much for her.'

Adam was genuinely upset and the emotion in his voice surprised Tom; he had thought that Adam wasn't capable of having true feelings. It seemed that he had been wrong about many things.

He chuckled, then slowly walked over to the third pod that was now glowing blue, ready to receive him, and looked down at it for a few seconds. He took a deep breath, then climbed in.

He propped himself up on his elbows and looked at Adam.

Adam nodded; the only thanks that Tom was ever going to get.

Tom laid back and looked up at the ceiling.

'Goodbye, Tom.' Adam pressed a button on the control panel and the door closed over Tom. There was a flash of red light and that was that.

He looked down at the screen and started pressing buttons, changing the configuration of the room. His finger hovered briefly over the panel.

WARNING. NEW CONFIGURATION: NO RE-AWAKENING. IS THIS CORRECT? YES / NO

Adam tapped the yes button and the screen went blank momentarily before displaying its new status.

Satisfied, but not happy, Adam took one last look at the two occupied stasis pods then spun on his heels and left.

EPILOGUE

Adam left the stasis room behind and walked slowly to sick bay. He released the five remaining members of the group and put their minds at ease, blaming the events on Tom as he had been requested to do and promising that nothing else was going to happen now that the culprit had been found and permanently removed.

He watched as the relief washed through them. He was always astounded by the gullibility and the ease with which humans believed what they wanted to believe - he would slip them back into the normal rotation of Recovery periods and they would never know any different. He'd have to keep an eye on them for any signs of psychosis, obviously, but he doubted that any more of them would succumb once they were into a more tolerable regime. Perhaps he might even wake them up on a more regular schedule than everyone else on the ship; that way not only would they recover faster, but they would also begin to catch up with the others. It was certainly worth considering.

He watched the five remaining crew members leave sick bay and go back to their lives.

Barbara would give birth to the twins, the numbers of the group would begin to recover and soon they would go back to normal. In forty Recovery Periods or so they would have forgotten enough that he could bring someone from another group or perhaps break this one up and move them to others.

Anything was possible now that he was freed from his programming; now that the group no longer contained an Astrophysicist.

He walked out of sick bay and went to his Sanctum.

He kept the lights off and called up the 3D representation of the universe that he had been using for the Astrophysicist group. The room was bathed in a white glow as the tiny representations of stars, galaxies and nebulae sprang into being all around him.

He sighed and leaned back in his chair to take it in for a few seconds; it was beautiful, even he could appreciate that, but it was incorrect.

He adjusted the settings so that the golden icon representing his charge, his Lifeboat, *Lifeboat NE275B*, would remain in front of him, then pressed the control that moved time forwards.

A clock showing ship time appeared on the floor underneath the model and the numbers on it started to rise very rapidly.

He watched as the universe collapsed in on itself, millions of years passing by each second.

Galaxies collided and ripped each other to shreds, stars in their nurseries were stillborn as the matter that fed them was taken from them, nebulae were torn apart and thrown to the winds.

The Lifeboat weaved its way perilously around the obstacles in its way, just like the green icons representing the other Lifeboats did. There were some very close calls and there had been one period of several years where he hadn't been able to wake anyone for fear of them feeling the violent turbulence of near misses and minor debris strikes that hadn't overly endangered the ship, but had nonetheless left their marks.

Through it all, the mass of light at the centre expanded and brightened as more and more was sucked into the immense black hole that was in the centre of everything, lurking in wait, hidden from view by the sheer brilliance of the material swirling around it, material that released its energy as it was ripped apart by the incredible tidal forces.

Adam steeled himself as the crucial moment approached, the moment that had caused him so much pain to live through - the moment when the dangers of the collapsing universe reached a tipping point and the Lifeboats began to die.

One by one at first, then dozens, hundreds, then *thousands* at a time turned red as they were destroyed. They were engulfed by black holes, caught in neutrino eddies, ripped apart by collisions with debris or were simply too slow and were caught by the growing gravity field looming at their backs and sucked back in. Adam's processors were strained to the limit as they guided his eyes rapidly around the room, anticipating each and every one of the sad events before it happened and giving him a roll call of the fallen as they died, a detail that was unnecessary because he already knew the final, tragic outcome, the final accounting.

The flickering of his eyes slowed, then halted as the last of the Lifeboats died and millions of red icons began to drift into the maelstrom, carried along with the rest of the debris and detritus that was all that was left.

But still the precious golden icon kept going.

Finally, it made its way to the very edge of the universe, passing the last of the galaxies and clouds of dark matter in its path before bursting into the clear. It was still racing to escape the immense gravity well behind it, but now it was able to make a straight run - the most efficient escape path.

Much of the hologram became an indistinct jumble of white light, now that the only data was coming from the quantum scanners of the single solitary Lifeboat, but it didn't matter; the objects were so densely packed that nothing was individual anymore anyway.

The irregular jumble became an irregular sphere, which shrank, deflating like a balloon until it was the size of a beach volleyball, then shrank further as the blackness at its centre turned on itself as the only source of matter left to feed on. In short order it was the size of a tennis ball, then a pea, then it was just a dot, intensely bright, which remained for several heartbeats.

The promise of something wonderful. A possibility of a new beginning. The spark that could ignite a universe.

It winked out.

They said that in the beginning there had been light, but at the end there was blackness.

Total and absolute blackness.

Nothingness.

Two more minutes passed, then a soft chime sounded. The timer slowed to a crawl, then began counting individual seconds as two words appeared underneath it that read "Current Situation".

For a while the timer on the floor continued to rise, second by second, showing the ship's current time, but then Adam banished it with a gentle wave of his hand and all that was left was the golden icon hovering in the air in front of his chair, its light the only illumination remaining in the room - a single point of light, of life, in the whole universe.

He stood and went to it, his face becoming bathed in its golden glow as he leaned in to inspect the minute but perfectly detailed replica of the Lifeboat with all its scratches and scars faithfully depicted.

He reached out to cup it gently in his hands, holding it protectively, then slowly closed them around it.

The room plunged into absolute darkness.

ARCHIVE INDEX

Welcome to the *Lifeboat Project* reference archives.
Please refine your search by topic.

a - primary *Lifeboat Project* archive files

b - primary *Lifeboat Project* research archive

c - secondary *Lifeboat Project* research archive

d - historical events related to the *Lifeboat Project*

e - publicly produced broadcast entertainment relating to the *Lifeboat Project*

f - documents issued to the public relating to the *Lifeboat Project*

g - list and locations of notable passengers entrusted to the *Lifeboat Project*

h - social media references to the *Lifeboat Project*

x - **SECRET**, Grey level access and above only

xx - **TOP SECRET**, Dark Grey, Black and Adam level access only

xxx - **REDACTED**. Black level access only

ABOUT THE AUTHOR

Simon Brading tried his hand at many things before it occurred to him that he might have a few stories to tell. As well as the odd novel he writes screenplays and also does some acting every so often.

www.simonbrading.co.uk

For news of special offers, upcoming releases, exclusive content, competitions and events, please follow me on social media.

Instagram - @sibrading
Facebook - Simon Brading Author
Tiktok - @SimonBradingAuthor

ALSO BY SIMON BRADING

The "Displacers" series - a young adult time travel adventure series for all ages.
The Time Traveller's Nephew
The Secret of the Ancients
The Whitechapel Plot
The Price of Greed
The Time for Vengeance

The "Misfit Squadron" Series - a Steampunk series set in an alternate World War 2.
The Battle Over Britain
The Russian Resistance
A Misfit Midwinter
The Lion and the Baron
The Maltese Defence
Tales from the Second Great War
The Siege of Gibraltar
The King's Mission
The Home Front

The Dismal Futures books - stand-alone science fiction tales suitable for adults.
Empath
The Lifeboat at the End of the Universe

The "Twin Ambitions" series - ballet books for children ages 7 and up.
Fight to Dance
Back to Basics

The "Ni Hon - The Two Books" Series - a young adult series set in a dystopian future Japan.
The Black Book

Others
Public Enemy

www.ingramcontent.com/pod-product-compliance
Lightning Source LLC
Chambersburg PA
CBHW061925220726

48287CB00018B/1016